The Prospect

Michelle Winn

authorHOUSE®

AuthorHouse™
1663 Liberty Drive
Bloomington, IN 47403
www.authorhouse.com
Phone: 1-800-839-8640

First published by AuthorHouse 11/23/2011

ISBN: 978-1-4634-2731-3 (sc)
ISBN: 978-1-4634-2730-6 (e)

Library of Congress Control Number: 2011910121

Printed in the United States of America

Chapter 1

The alarm clock sounded off loudly in Haylee Jones's ear at what seemed to be too early an hour. The sun was already starting to peek through her curtains in bright shades of orange, but she wasn't ready to get up. She never considered herself a morning person, but unfortunately, sometimes her job required it. And it did that morning.

Rising, she walked to the large windows of her bedroom in her downtown Indianapolis townhouse. Pushing the velvet, rose-colored drapes aside, she glanced at the street below to watch the people rushing to start their day. Sometimes she could sit for hours just observing, wondering where people were going and what they would be doing. If she was going to be prompt for her appointment, there was no time for that today. She headed to her kitchen for coffee.

After brewing a pot and eating a small breakfast, Haylee flipped open her day planner. She glanced over her schedule for the day, looking forward to the last thing she had written toward the bottom. 'Dinner with Kathy at Harmony', it said. A girls night out would be a great end to the busy Friday she had planned.

She took a long shower then quickly dressed. Seeing the clock had counted down to mere minutes before she needed to leave, Haylee hurried out to her Jeep Wrangler parked in the garage below her building. If she had been the kind to fuss over her appearance, she would never be on time. Luckily, she had a creamy skin tone and large, bright brown eyes that did not require much makeup. She kept her brown hair trimmed above her shoulders so that it took five minutes flat to blow-dry and style. Her wardrobe was functional and simplistic, never adhering to fashion fads, but clung to her tall, slim frame seamlessly. Though she had no clue, her natural type of beauty easily attracted people to her.

Traffic was light on the way to the office, but she didn't have far to go to make it there. She had just enough time to gather up her paperwork into a file before she went to the closing at eight. She worked at Baxter Realty, a local real estate company, as a realtor. The job kept her energized, she enjoyed interacting with the variety of people she came into contact with, and it gave her the flexibility for the social life she desired.

Walking in the front doors, she immediately saw Bob behind the front desk. Smiling to herself, she snuck up to the counter while he had his back turned and said "Um, excuse me. I am looking to sell my home and I need some immediate assistance."

Bob whirled around, startled that someone had come up behind him without him hearing it. His anxiety that had arisen from the tone of voice turned into relief when he saw it was Haylee. Just as fast as his alarm had subsided, his nerves kicked in.

"Oh, hi Ms. Jones. You surprised me. I thought I was about to get into trouble again."

"How many times do I have to ask you to call me Haylee?"

"I guess you will have to keep telling me. I think my Dad would like it better if I called you Ms. Jones. That way I get used to addressing everyone, including clients, more formally."

"Well, I might just have to try to talk some sense into him."

Fresh out of high school, Bob had just started working at the office his Dad owned, expected to follow in his father's footsteps. He had more than a little crush on Haylee, and it made him fumble when she came around. His Dad was already getting on him for some errors he had been making, so he was trying his best to concentrate and focus.

"You've had a few phone calls already this morning. I sent them to your voicemail."

"Okay Bob, thanks. See you later."

Haylee rounded the corner and headed to her desk. She waved at some of the other associates on her way there, taking stock of the appearances of her colleagues. It looked as though Sally had begun her morning in a frazzle, which was quite typical. Joe was busy sweet-talking a client on the telephone as he smiled and waved back at Haylee, while Jane was cursing at the fax machine for not working properly. Haylee kept moving since Sally was already on her way over to help Jane, though reluctantly and not without rolling her eyes.

She sat down in her cushioned chair parked behind her corner cubicle. Organized chaos some might call it, but she certainly knew where everything was situated in her tiny space of the office. Compared to some of the other agents, she completely thought her desk could be described as nothing short of exceedingly tidy. A few select pictures hung on the bulletin board in front of her, along with her favorite, and decidedly inspirational, poem. Post-it notes scribbled with reminders lined the right wall surrounding her desk, while listing sheets of the houses she had for sale crowded the left. The file she needed was perched atop a pile of paperwork, and least no one in their right mind could call her paperwork anything but meticulous. She shuffled it all to the side and pulled her phone forward.

Her first message was from a client saying that he wasn't sure if he wanted to make an offer on the property they had viewed the prior evening. She sighed to herself, thinking how typical that was of a first-time homebuyer. She had come to learn how to deal with those kinds of situations, gently persuading clients to go with their first instincts.

Not one to be pushy, she treated her clients the way she would want had their places been reversed. She took on the role of an information provider, only presenting guided influence when necessary. Though she was the expert, she wanted her clients to make educated decisions without much persuasion from her. It was, ultimately, their financial burden to take on.

She assured herself she would resolve that client's snag by the end of the day.

The next message was from her friend Kathy, reminding Haylee to call her after work so they could figure out what time to meet each other that evening.

The last was the one that bothered her. It was from Dave, the friendly yet overbearing acquaintance of Kathy's. Kathy was always trying to set her up on dates despite her insistent refusals. No matter how many times Haylee told her not to, Kathy did so anyway. And Haylee wound up going on those dates, but worse yet, didn't have the heart to them if she wasn't interested. She tended to ignore subsequent phone calls until they fell by the wayside.

As she listened to Dave profess the good time he had with her, she shifted uncomfortably in her chair. She couldn't see anything more than a friendship developing between them, though she knew from his words that was not his intention. Relationships in the romantic form did not work well with her. Pressing the delete button, she thought to herself that she had to remember not to give her business card out in those instances.

The closing she attended had been through a title company that was located in the same building as the real estate company she worked for. After it was over, she spent her time calling clients and preparing marketing materials for the rest of the morning. Then it was off to a closing that afternoon. It ran a little longer than expected, but was completed nonetheless, which was the important part. Having finished all she had planned for the workday, she decided to hit the gym for a quick workout before returning Kathy's call. A short run on the treadmill was all she needed.

The hardest part of working out, in her mind, was not only finding the time but the motivation. Getting up in the morning before heading off to work was not an option since she was always too groggy to even think about moving around prematurely. She usually tried to fit it in right after work, but some nights she was entirely too drained. This evening, she had both the time and the motivation so she took advantage of it before she talked herself out of it.

When she arrived at Basic Fitness, she was happy to see the cardio area of the center nearly empty. She hustled to the locker room, knowing she would have to change her clothes in a hurry if she wanted to beat the rush of people that would swarm in right after five o'clock. It was so frustrating to have to wait to get on a machine, which would probably have happened had she come about fifteen minutes later. The longer she waited, the shorter her visit there would become.

The center was small, packed tight with only a handful of treadmills, ellipticals, Stairmasters, and weight machines. Right after business hours was its busiest time, and the only time Haylee could normally come. But for the price she paid for membership, combined with her track record of low attendance, she couldn't bring herself to spend more at a larger facility.

A feature of the facility that she couldn't do without was the fact that it kept a stock of magazines handy for the patrons to read. Currently, the bin contained the latest copy of *Glamour*, so she plucked it from the stack and hopped on a treadmill right in front of a television. The set in front of her was showing music videos and the corresponding songs were on the speakers overhead. One way or another, she was determined to distract herself from the timer on the machine that counted down the long thirty minutes until she was finished. The stint went by much faster when she didn't constantly watch the clock.

To her chagrin, the belt below her feet was slowing to a stop before she knew it.

Haylee weaved through the mass of people, flipping open her cell phone as she strolled out of the building. Kathy answered on the second ring.

"Hey, what're you doing?"

"I made a pit stop at the gym. I finished work a little early today."

"Oh. Well, that's not on *my* agenda today. Quite the opposite. I'm ready for a cocktail."

"I'll bet." When the two of them had made plans, Kathy had warned her that she might be a little stressed by the end of the day. One of her fellow employees had abruptly needed time off, and being one of the managers, Kathy had been roped into covering for her. A twelve-hour shift at the retail store she worked was enough to send her nerves flying. She only had so much patience per day, and when it was used up she could get testy. It was even worse when she had days where it was depleted within the first few hours of a shift due to difficult customers.

"So I take it you need to have an evening of fun to make you feel better?"

"No, I just want to sit at home on the couch tonight, alone, and twiddle my thumbs." She paused before sarcastically asking, "What do you think?"

"Alright, don't get your skirt in a twist. You want to come pick me up? I am walking in my front door as we speak, and I should be ready to go in about an hour."

"Sure, I'll see you then."

"Okay, bye."

From years of being acquainted, Haylee and Kathy knew each very well. They shared many common interests, but their differences made their friendship unique. In many regards, they were like night and day in personality. Kathy was straightforward, sometimes brash, and headstrong; Haylee was more easygoing, overtly kind with words, and unassuming. Haylee was gullible while Kathy was leery. Kathy thrived in amorous relationships, and Haylee steered clear of them. While most would gravitate toward people similar to them, the two of them found each other complementary.

Kathy turned up as promised an hour later. She let herself in Haylee's home, walking straight to the bathroom where she figured Haylee would be finishing up.

"I thought you told me you were going to start locking that front door at all times?"

"Oh yeah. Well, I knew you would be here any minute anyway." She peered over Kathy's shoulder to the wall clock in the adjoining bedroom. "Right on time actually."

"You won't be saying 'oh yeah' when someone waltzes in here and beats you. Or worse."

"Yeah, yeah I know. I'm working on it."

"And you better finish up. Our reservation is in thirty minutes."

Since it was essentially her second home, Kathy went into Haylee's kitchen, delving into the refrigerator in search of a drink. She had to shake her head with disapproval when she looked inside and saw the contents. "What did this girl eat?" she thought to herself. No wonder she stays slim, nothing but condiments in here. There did happen to be a half bottle of unfinished pinot grigio on the top shelf, but there was no telling how old it might be. Kathy half expected to find a cobweb attached to her hand, proving the appliance had not been opened in some time. Pulling the cork out of the wine, she took a whiff, decided it was indeed still good, and had a small sip to confirm it.

There was a recent picture of the two of them, held in place by a magnet on the side of the refrigerator that Kathy noticed while she reached into a cabinet for wine glasses.

"Can you make me a copy of that one when you get a chance?" Kathy asked Haylee when she joined her in the room.

"Sure, just remind me," Haylee told her as she scooped up the wine that had been poured for her. "So tell me about this new love interest I have yet to meet while we sip these."

Beaming with obvious delight, Kathy replied, "Think I got a good one. He's a good balance to me, and we have a lot of fun together. His name is Jake. You'll meet him soon."

"No doubt. He wouldn't be able to avoid me forever."

"True. So, did Dave call you this week?"

Exasperated, Haylee rolled her eyes. "Yeah he did. What's it to ya?"

"Any interest?"

"Not really. He was polite and all but I don't think he is for me. We could have a decent friendship. But that's about it."

Now it was Kathy's turn to roll her eyes. "That's all you ever say."

"Because that's the way it happens. I'm too busy right now anyway."

"How are you ever going to find someone if you don't make the time? Or make the effort for that matter."

Haylee bit her lip as she swirled the last remaining drops of wine around in her glass. The answer to that question eluded her. She avoided serious relationships like a plague, though not always purposely. Knowing she did so did not remedy the problem. She had tried, obviously unsuccessfully, to overcome the trauma of her past. As a child, the ordeal had seemed so large, but now, trivial. A mere speed bump in her life. But somehow, those fears still steered her.

"I don't know. Maybe he'll just magically appear," she said with more hope than sarcasm. Haylee rinsed her glass before setting beside the sink. "Let's get out of here before we lose our table."

"Fine, change the subject." Kathy pivoted on her heel, turning around when she was outside. "And don't forget to lock that damn door behind you."

Chapter 2

~~~~~~~~~~~~~~~~~~~~~~~~~~~~~~~

The air was cooler that evening, but still warm enough that Kathy rolled the car windows down on their way to Harmony. The restaurant had just opened a few weeks prior, and so far had great reviews. They were anxious to get their take on it.

The leaves were beginning to change colors in preparation for the fall season. Haylee admired the red, gold, and orange shades as they drove down the street. Day was giving way to night, and the sky was growing darker by the minute. Street lights were beginning to flicker on, illuminating the city with artificial light. The air held the aroma of fresh rain from the dousing the clouds sent earlier that evening.

Kathy popped a Rolling Stones disc in her player and the women sang along with the music at a low volume, reluctant to be heard by passing traffic.

Upon arrival, the pair only waited a few minutes for their table. The list of choices the menu offered was small, making their decisions easier, so they had already decided when someone came to take their order. Haylee chose the salmon special and Kathy opted for the filet with a red wine demi-glace.

The décor inside was modern and very well done. It was apparent that the designers understood the value in a restaurant that was comfortable yet still looked sleek. The light fixtures cast a subtle luminosity down to the tables with their opaque, bowl-shaped coverings. The dim glow helped to offset the rich, cream-colored walls that were dotted with mosaic paintings throughout. White linen cloths covered every table, and high-backed, padded chairs were pushed in beneath them. The main dining room was one big open area, but the tables were far enough apart so that it didn't feel too crowded.

The dull roar of activity surrounding them forced Haylee and Kathy to raise their voices while they nibbled on the crusty bread that had been placed between them. The time it took to get their meals was short, or at least seemed short because they talked nonstop. The food was tasty and well prepared in a perfectly portioned size. They chose to skip dessert since they were too full from their entrees.

Adjacent to the main dining room was a bar area with a small dance floor. The space around the bar counter was already filled with patrons so they found themselves having to stand to the side of it while they waited for the live band to finish setting up. They sipped their drinks and watched as a few brave souls danced to the CD that was currently blaring from the speakers. Before they could decide whether or not to join in, Haylee noticed a tall, male stranger hurrying toward them. And was surprised when Kathy gave him a big hug.

"Haylee, this is who I told you about. This is Jake."

"Nice to meet you," Haylee gasped out as Jake proceeded to squeeze her in a bear hug.

"Likewise. I have heard a lot about you. Kathy has been anxious for us to meet."

Haylee smirked at her friend. "She told you all good things I hope."

"Well….mostly," he trailed off. He laughed when her eyes narrowed. Jake's sense of humor was playful, and he had been told Haylee could take teasing in stride. "I'm kidding, of course."

Haylee snickered. "I can already see you guys are two peas in a pod."

The silent exchange between the new couple was drenched in admiration. Kathy asked Haylee, "Do you mind if I chat with Jake for a minute? He can't stay long. We'll do the 'getting to know you' thing another time."

"Not at all."

"We're going to step outside so we can actually *hear* each other." Kathy said immediately after the band started playing.

"I'll try to get us some seats while you're gone."

As they walked away, Haylee eyed two chairs being vacated by patrons and hurried over to them, knowing Kathy wouldn't leave her hanging alone long.

He had followed her over to where she now sat and tapped her lightly on the shoulder to get her attention. Haylee swiveled around in her seat and was faced with someone that looked vaguely familiar, though she couldn't quite place who he was.

He gestured to the stool next to her. "May I?"

She shrugged. "Sure. Until my friend gets back."

After he was comfortable, he continued. "Don't you work at Baxter Realty?"

Haylee hesitated as she searched her mind for how she knew him. "Yes. Do I know you?"

"Well, no. I thought I had recognized you from there. I

have been in a few times to visit Bob, keep an eye on him. He is my cousin. Actually more like a younger brother."

"Oh, I see. I'm sure you have seen me running around the office then." She extended her hand. "What is your name?"

"Scott Myer," he said as he grasped her hand in return.

"Haylee Jones."

"Do want something to drink, Haylee?"

"I would." Even sitting right next to him, Haylee was hard pressed to hear. Nevertheless, it was nice to have someone to keep her company while Kathy was off with Jake.

The bar was incredibly busy and when it was their turn to order, the bartender just pointed to the two of them to get their preferences.

"Vodka tonic, extra lime."

"I'll have a glass of chardonnay please." Haylee told him.

He darted off, but quickly returned with two glasses.

"How long have you worked at Baxter?"

"Just over a year. It's a really good company." She sipped her beer. "How about you, what do you do?"

"I'm in sales as well, for medical supplies. Similar to real estate in a way, in that it's all about relationships." Haylee nodded in agreement. "Are you from around here?" he continued.

"I am. Excluding the four years of college, I've always lived here." She watched as he poked and prodded the limes in his glass with his straw.

"The area is relatively new to me. I went to school in New York, then worked in the city for awhile before coming here."

"A bit of a change, I imagine. Why the move?"

"Work. A position opened here, offering more pay, even

with the cost of living being so much lower. Hard to turn down."

While they carried on, Haylee had a chance to study him. He was charming, as evidenced by his engaging expressions and subtle complements. The air of confidence surrounding him was thick, but thus far not offensive. His dark hair was long enough on top that Haylee could picture herself running her fingers through it, even if slightly hindered by the gel glossing over the strands. The eyes that lazily drifted over her as they spoke were the same auburn color of the tresses above them. He was built in such a way that Haylee guessed that he liked to lift weights in his spare time. It was fair to say she was attracted to him.

When Kathy had finally rejoined Haylee, she excused herself for interrupting.

Haylee snuck a peak at the time on her watch. She had not realized how much time had passed with Scott while she had waited for Kathy. "I wasn't keeping track, but I'd say you were gone more than a minute or two."

"True. But when I came back inside, I could see that you were pleasantly busy. So I coaxed Jake into staying a bit longer." Much longer in fact. It was now late enough that Kathy grew tired from her long day. "Are you about ready to go? I'm beat," she confessed.

"Yeah. Give me a minute, I'll meet you out front." She turned back to Scott. "I've got to go. It was nice to meet you, I had a good time," she told him as she rose from her seat.

"Mind if I call you sometime?" Scott probed.

"Yes. Err..No…I mean I don't mind," she blurted. It was a question she tended to shy away from, but oddly, she hadn't felt inclined to in this case.

After writing her number down for him and saying good-bye, Haylee headed to the parking lot to find Kathy waiting at the curb in her car. She caught a glimpse of Kathy yawning, before her attention was drawn to the vehicle pulling up behind them. After her vision adjusted from the headlights, she could recognize Jake as he waved to her.

Haylee climbed into the passenger side and pulled the seatbelt over her right shoulder. "Looks like you are having company tonight?"

Kathy was wiping the tears that had formed from yawing so hard. "Wow, you're very observant." She glanced in the rearview mirror. "We are going to watch a movie."

"Is that what you are calling it?"

The corner of Kathy's mouth curved upward. "Well, it's not code for something else."

"You are going to fall asleep the instant you sit on that couch."

Kathy laughed, "So, what of it? Mind your own business." Unlike her friend, Kathy did not shy away from male companionship, but embraced it. She made her choices wisely, but figured if she was to get hurt that was just part of the game. And if it was meant to be, somehow it would work out.

"Let's change the subject over to you. Who was that guy you were talking to?"

"He's related to someone that works in my office. He kept me company while you ditched me."

Pretending to be insulted, Kathy exclaimed, "I didn't ditch you! I wouldn't have stepped out if you hadn't wanted me to." She cracked her window to let in some cool air before she got sleepy at the wheel. "Are you going to talk to him again?"

"Probably. I gave him my number. So you can go ahead and be impressed and not give me a hard time about it." Haylee was certain that was coming next.

"Fair enough. Tell me about him."

"He's new to the area, transferred positions in his

company. He's a medical supplies sales rep. I found him attractive and easy to talk to."

"Sounds like a good start."

"We'll see." Haylee tilted her head back on the seat rest, feeling the weight of exhaustion sinking in. "What do you have planned for tomorrow? I am going shopping to buy a few things for the condo if you want to tag along."

"Mmmm, can't. Jake and I are going hiking tomorrow. We both love the fall season. I only hope he's not taking me to some extremely challenging path. Otherwise, he might be carrying me back. Physical exertion is not high on my entertainment list."

Kathy would not call herself anything remotely close to athletic. She much preferred to watch sporting events than to participate in them. As for exercise, she did the bare minimum, solely for health reasons. If it were at all possible to maintain good physical condition with only her social activities, she would be all about it.

"Do you want to borrow my hiking boots?" Haylee wondered.

"No, I'll be fine in my sneakers. It's not like we are going to the mountains."

"You'd be surprised the difference shoes can make."

Kathy threw the car in park at the curb in front of Haylee's home. "If my dogs are barking that bad then I'll coax Jake into massaging them. That'll teach him a lesson."

Jake's headlights were falling in line with Kathy's car as Haylee glanced back. "I guess it would. Have fun."

"Will do. Sleep tight."

She barely had the energy, but Haylee managed to drag herself to her bathroom to wash her face and brush her teeth. She pulled on a comfortable pair of flannel pajamas before crawling under the down comforter on top of her queen size bed. It was soothing to know the alarm was not set to wake her in the morning. She had the entire weekend free of anything work-related, which was rare.

Most often, it was difficult to sustain a Monday-through-Friday schedule when so many of her clients were only free on the weekends. She would work to accommodate them, but wished she had more Saturdays and Sundays to herself. It was a common struggle in her profession, and a battle she often lost in the name of customer service. But she tolerated it because there were many other aspects of her job she did like.

At that hour, it was very quiet in her home. It was the nights, when she readied herself for bed, when she was reminded of the solitary lifestyle she leads, one she inflicted upon herself. During the day she surrounded herself with people, went to dinner with friends, or had them over. But in the last intimate hours before sleep, she only had her own thoughts.

Once the sleep timer was set on the small television on top of her dresser, Haylee drifted off, but not to slumber. Her mind mulled over her evening, and therefore over Scott as well. It had been a pleasant chance encounter. She doubted anything would come of it, but she relished the fact that she felt comfortable in his presence, had been undaunted by his advances. She would willingly accept an invitation from him, if it was provided, without the normal uncertainty and caution.

There was hope for her yet.

Chapter 3

~~~~~~~~~~~~~~~~~~~~~~~~~~~~~~~~~~

$\mathcal{H}$aylee arose midmorning, showered, and was out the door in an hour. She had placed a cap over her head and pulled on jeans and a snug-fitting T-shirt. She was anxious to get out, shop, and pick up a few things for her condo. It had only been about three months since she moved in and the place was still fairly barren. The small apartment she had occupied for the last several years had little room for furniture. Comparatively, in her new, open space, it appeared as though she hadn't owned anything.

Eventually, she wanted to be able to have small groups over for dinner and at least do some entertaining. At the moment, the necessary furniture and dishware to accomplish that did not occupy her home, so she was out in search of it. All the purchases she needed or wanted to make would have to be a slow, sporadic process due to cash flow. But she had made some priorities and was decidedly tired of eating at the coffee table.

She had considered walking to shops since they weren't far from her townhouse, but thought better of it because she would need a way to transport anything she bought. Plus, rain was in the forecast, despite the sky showing no signs of a downpour.

Haylee decided to first try a used furniture shop two blocks down the street. It was her hope to find a discarded dining set with life still in it. The practical side of her did not see the need to acquire all of her first real furnishings brand new.

She was pleased when she discovered an oak table with little wear that wouldn't even need refinishing. The table included sleeves to extend it when she had guests over, and a set of eight chairs. A few of the chairs would have to be stored in the garage because of limited space, but for the price, she decided to go ahead and get them all so that she had them if need be. The clerk at the store took her money and promised they could have the set delivered to her by Monday free of charge. She managed to stay under budget *and* wouldn't have to worry about finding a way to transport the pieces.

Haylee made additional thoughtful purchases in her subsequent stops. She picked up a dishware set that had been more expensive than anticipated, even on sale. Had it not been discounted, she would have passed on it—the mismatched plates and glasses in her cabinets weren't so bad. But the cute swirl design in black and white had been exactly what she had wanted, and she bought them before she gave herself a chance to change her mind.

After she found the oversized throw rug in a similar black-and-white pattern, she resolved to be done for the day. The rug, intended to be placed on the laminate flooring under the dining table, wasn't exactly necessary, but more of an impulse buy. Her purchases, normally carefully calculated, caused her the slightest bit of angst over the dollars she had spent. She vowed not to return anything, trusting she had made good choices. One room of the condo was done, at least for the moment.

When she arrived home, she had a message on her voicemail. The recorded voice was quickly recognized as Scott's. He very cordially asked if he could take Haylee out for dinner the following Friday. It was unexpected that he had called so soon, but Haylee concluded that she must have made an impression. Smiling, she picked up the phone to return his call. She couldn't believe she was actually getting excited by the date prospect. He answered on the first ring.

"Hello?"

"Hi. Is Scott available?"

"This is." He paused only a second. "Is this Haylee?"

Taken aback, she answered, "Yeah, how did you know?"

"It's that great invention called caller ID. I only called you a moment ago, too."

Duh. Obviously, her mind was muddled enough for her basic reasoning skills to go down the drain. "Right. I'm a little slow today.....not enough coffee."

"I've had plenty." After having been up so late the night before, he had needed it all. "Since you called back, I assume you are going to accept my invitation?"

Confident and straightforward, she thought. Then again, it made sense that she would just ignore the message had she meant to decline.

"Sure. Where do you want to go?"

"Don't worry about that, I'll take care of it. I asked you after all." He waited, but she offered no resistance. He was right to assume she would oblige. "I'll pick you up at six."

"Okay. 1425 Spruce Street."

"Got it. I'll see you then."

"Alright. Bye."

Scott was smirking as he hung up the phone. The office Haylee worked in was small, and therefore, information spread like wildfire. Bob had been kind enough that morning to pass along what tidbits he had overheard when Scott had prompted him. It was said that she preferred to fly solo, refraining from the dating arena. It presented Scott with a small challenge that he wanted to embrace, even if it took more coaxing than he liked to give. He gave himself a little credit for being more charismatic than he thought.

Work kept Haylee busy the following week, and it was Friday before she knew it. She almost regretted making plans for the night, particularly considering the scope of the event, and she considered calling Scott and cancelling. She was in the mood to sit on her couch and read a book or watch a movie. But courtesy won out, especially since a last-minute cancellation would add an extra serving of rudeness.

The destination for dinner had not been provided to her, so Haylee dressed casually. The nights were getting cooler so she chose dark jeans and a long-sleeved red sweater that went well with her favorite silver hoop earrings. She pulled her hair back in a ponytail because she couldn't muster the motivation to do anything else with it, but she did freshen up her lipstick and eyeliner.

She felt frazzled. It had been a long, taxing week, and she was struggling to find any reserved energy. On top of that, for reasons she couldn't quite explain, she was nervous. She had to remind herself that this was supposed to be fun, without pressure, but it hardly relieved the tension.

To distract herself, she straightened up the kitchen while she waited for Scott to arrive. The doorbell rang right as she had finished emptying the dishwasher.

"Good start at least," she said aloud to herself, noting that he came on time. Occasionally she struggled to be prompt herself, so she respected the trait in others.

When she opened the door, Haylee was impressed to see that he had brought her yellow lilies, her favorite flower. "Hi! How did you know?"

"Know what?" he asked with a sly grin.

"That these are my favorite flowers?"

"Lucky guess?"

Haylee raised an eyebrow. "Really?"

"Alright, no," Scott admitted. "Bob told me."

"Well thank you. They're beautiful."

He nodded. "Are you all set to go?"

"Yeah, let me just grab my purse."

"Great." Admittedly, he was pleased he would not have to wait while she finished getting ready.

"So where are we going? Or do I have to wait and see when we get there?"

"We are going to Blue Ocean first and then to S and G's for a show."

"Good choices." Seafood and comedy sat well with her.

"I figured anyone could appreciate a good laugh."

"I could use one. I've had a long day."

Scott gestured toward his car and Haylee circled around the opposite side.   She instinctively wrinkled her nose when she got in. There had been a half-hearted attempt to cover the smell, but the scent of cigarette smoke was heavy in the air. The obvious question was on the tip of her tongue, but then she saw the pack lying on the console between them.

When he picked them up, she was watching him. "Want one?" he asked.

"Oh, no thanks." It was one habit she could never

acquire. Aside from health reasons, being in close quarters with the smoke flat out made her nauseous.

"Would it bother you if I did?" When she hesitated, he merely put the car in gear, refraining for the time being.

"Thanks." She crossed her ankles and turned her body toward his. "So how has your week been?"

"Uhh, good. Nothing too exciting. I did get to see my older brother the other day. I had to drive up to Chicago to meet with a potential new account. He had the night free so he took me out before I headed home."

"Does he live downtown?"

"Yeah. Has a place right next to the river. It's small though, smaller than my apartment, even the one I had in New York. I don't know how he makes do with it, but he claims more space would only be more to clean. Me, I don't like to feel closed in."

"I prefer some leg room as well, but to each his own." She cringed as Scott sped up to catch the light yellow, barely getting through without it being a blatant run of red. "Is he your only one? Brother, I mean."

"Nope, I have a younger one that's in his senior year of college. Pre-med. Gonna be in school forever. He'll be doing his second four years here in town."

"Oh wow. That'll be nice for you all to be in close proximity."

"Yeah. But I doubt we'll see a lot of each other, we'll all be pretty busy."

Haylee thought it would be great to even have the option. "At least the opportunity will be there. I don't have that choice. I'm an only child. I've always envied people that had bigger families. Growing up, I missed having someone in the house to play with, or talk with, that was around my age."

"Or if you had my family, fight with."

"Fight with?" She hadn't contemplated that.

"My brothers and I beat up on each other all the time. Mom had a hell of a time trying to pry us apart. We would leave all kinds of marks on one another. Maybe that's why Max is going to med school, to learn how to heal all those wounds we gave him." He chuckled. "Since he was the youngest and the smallest, he got the worst of it. It was all in good fun though."

Haylee was shaking her head in hilarity when Scott glanced over at her. She shouldn't have been surprised by the confession of constant roughhousing.

"What? You didn't think we played with dolls did you?"

"Well no, of course not. I guess the perspective is just different."

He patted the hand that rested on Haylee's leg. "We would have been cordial and sweet to sisters, had there been any."

Her arm instinctively wanted to pull her hand inward, away from Scott's, but she forced it to stay put. "I hope so. Genuine gentlemen, right?"

"Always."

Scott pulled up beside the curb adjacent to the restaurant. He stepped out of the vehicle so that the valet could step in and helped Haylee out of the other side of the car. He led her inside and she stood next to him when they approached the hostess stand.

The young girl behind the stand gave them a wide smile.

"Hello, how are you doing tonight?" she inquired.

"Good," Scott replied bluntly. "I had a reservation for two under Bell."

"Okay." She typed into the touch screen computer in front of her, a frown slowly forming on her face. "For what time?" she asked in the same pleasant tone as her first question.

"Six-thirty."

Haylee watched as the hostess scanned the information in front of her, her brow furrowed.

"I'm sorry, I'm not finding it…." she trailed off.

Scott could feel a twinge of impatience. "I called earlier in the week and was told I was all set for tonight."

"Hmmm. And you said Bill right?"

Scott huffed out his breath, quickly clearing his throat as a cover when he saw Haylee glance in his direction.

"No. It's Bell, with an 'e'."

"I apologize," she told him as she changed her error. "There you are, right this way."

After they had ordered, Scott was happy to answer Haylee's questions regarding his job. She listened intently, resting her chin in the palm of her hand. It wasn't often that she wasn't the one doing the talking, not because she was such a talker, but because she always seemed to be asked plenty of questions. And she wasn't a one-word answer type.

Nor was Scott. She had to admit, it was a nice change of pace to not have to feel as though she had to pull information out of him. He offered it freely. He had strong opinions concerning the operations of his company and told her he'd like to make the appropriate changes after he had worked his way to a position that allowed him to do so. It was a part of why he transferred offices. There wasn't anywhere for him to go if he stayed where he was. Money was the main determinant, he simply hadn't made enough, but he kept that to himself.

Haylee could appreciate a hard worker. She was one herself. And she liked that he was into weight-lifting, he had a nice build, though it seemed contradictory of the smoking tendency he possessed. Maybe it was an infrequent habit, or so she hoped.

The more he talked, the more commonalities there appeared to be between them. Of course, it didn't hurt that every time he flashed his captivating grin, he had Haylee automatically smiling, too.

Haylee instinctively tried to catch a glimpse of the check when it came so that she could offer her share. But Scott shooed her hand away before she had a chance to do so. She shifted uncomfortably in her chair, finding this part of any date decidedly awkward.

When they arrived at the show, Haylee insisted she cover their tickets. To her surprise, and chagrin, he did not argue but chose to placate her. She thought it was only fair.

Unintentionally, Scott won extra points for the entertainment. The amusement had been just what Haylee needed and it felt good to laugh so generously. The stand-up comedians had original material and were unreserved in their jabs. She did not mind the profanity because it was always inserted in such a way that it enhanced the jokes. However, she was relieved they had gotten there only minutes before the scheduled start time and had to get a seat in back. The patrons in the front row were picked on mercilessly, and Haylee did not envy their forced participation. At least they had been warned that would be the case up front she supposed.

As he drove her home, Haylee wondered what Scott's expectations were for the ending of the evening. She knew what hers were, and ultimately it really didn't matter what he wanted, but it would be easier if he didn't expect anything.

When they got to her house, he only asked if she would like him to walk her to the door, but she shook her head.

"No, that's alright, I'll be fine. Thanks for everything. I had a good time tonight."

He displayed his vast grin again as she exited the car. "Me too. I'll call you."

For once, she really hoped he meant it.

Chapter 4

Scott stunned Haylee when she got back to the office after lunch on Monday. He had left a note for her at the front desk while she had been gone, thanking her for a great evening. He also asked if she would like to get together that weekend, and to call him if she decided she wanted to. She didn't have any plans yet; however, she still didn't want to commit to it without some thought first. Her doubts were reemerging.

Later when she got home, Haylee called Kathy to see how her week was going. Naturally, Kathy couldn't resist.

"Didn't you go on a date with that guy over the weekend? What was his name?"

"Scott. And yes I did."

There was a pause, "And? How did it go?"

"It was fine. We went out for dinner, then went to a comedy club. We had quite a bit in common."

"That's it? It was fine?"

"Well yeah, what do you want me to say?"

Kathy audibly sighed. "Nothing I guess. You gonna see him again?"

"I don't know. He left me a note today at the office thanking me, and asked if I want to do something again. Not sure if I want to."

"Why not?" Kathy added, "I'm just curious."

Haylee fell back on the bed, threw her legs over the side. "For one, I'm very busy with work right now."

"Excuses. You work too much. Which is hard for me to understand since I count down the minutes to rush out of the office." She asked, "And for two?"

Haylee hadn't thought she would be asked, and realized she didn't currently have anymore reasons in mind. She searched for another answer.

"You don't have a two do you?"

"Yes. Maybe he's not my type."

"Lame reply. Nobody is your type." Kathy shifted the phone to her other ear, wanting to delve in deeper. "What about him isn't? The fact that you apparently had a lot in common? Oh no, no, I got it. You said he's good-looking. You're looking for someone that's harder on the eyes."

On the other end of the line, Haylee was sneering. "You know, you can really be a bitch. A royal pain in the ass."

Kathy was glowing with pride. "I know." She considered it a virtue rather than a fault. "You love that about me. Admit it."

There was an honestly between them that Haylee was fond of. She suspected Kathy could succeed at developing that direct nature with anyone, as long as they were even slightly open to it. However, some took it for outright rudeness.

"I would stop calling you if I didn't."

"Right." An experience that was not uncommon for her. Kathy took it in stride because she never intended to be mean, only forthright.

"Anyway, there are some points in his court at least. You

could get to know him a little better before you make any snap judgments."

"I suppose."

Haylee went to the kitchen after she had hung up the phone. Kathy made a good point that it couldn't hurt to become better acquainted with Scott before making any rash decisions about him. That would be harmless enough.

She began to pull ingredients from the refrigerator. She enjoyed cooking, but didn't get around to doing it enough. It was often late by the time she arrived home and taking the time out to make dinner didn't feel like an option. Being on the go, she frequently feasted anywhere but at home. But when time allowed, she took the opportunity to make a tasty meal, if only for herself.

She hummed to herself as she chopped onions, then broccoli. She preheated the oven while she seared the chicken, taking in the scent of garlic rising from the pan on the cooktop. The casserole she chose to make was easy and uncomplicated, and was inspired by items already in inventory in her kitchen. The last layer of the assembly was cheddar cheese, and she spread that over the top with a heavy hand. The recipe had been her mother's, and the aroma that expelled from the oven while it baked reminded her of childhood.

Recalling those days could either bring a smile to her face, or a pain to her heart, depending on the context of the memory. Her mother, to this day, was a kind, warm, and devoted person. She had always been there for Haylee, and she knew she could rely on her for anything. The other side of that coin was not as rosy, and Haylee did her best to keep those recollections to the back of her mind.

She settled in at the coffee table in front of the couch, even though her dining table now stood only a few feet away. Here, she had a better view of the television and she flipped to the channel showing her favorite sitcom. It took one scene for her to realize she had already seen that episode.

Her thoughts began to drift into the future. She could envision a picture of herself ten years from now, sitting on the same couch, alone, eating dinner. It was a bleak image, and unwanted at that. She craved companionship, but could not seem to give any effort toward gaining it.

At the base of it all was fear. She did not want to suffer the broken heart her mother did. She saw firsthand how it tore that woman apart, how it sucked the life out of her. Being witness to that created a defense mechanism in her, in the form of avoidance. She had decided long ago that, given the choice, she would rather dodge the bullet no matter how great the rewards appeared to be in the beginning. Once things got too personal, she would back away. The caveat was that she didn't want to be alone anymore.

She was pushing herself toward change. It wouldn't be easy, and she was unsure of the steps. However, she believed she had at least one attribute in her favor. Inside was dedication, as evidenced by her career. She would resolve to try instead of trying to run.

Before she could change her mind, the phone was in her hand, number already dialed. Scott sounded pleased when she accepted his invitation.

She gave herself a pat on the back for steps on the right path.

Haylee was not sure she believed love could endure years on end. She knew personally of examples when it hadn't. But in this ordinary evening, it had dawned on her that without an open heart, it would fail anyway. With the exception of family and friends, she would have the same outcome of solitude.

Before she went to meet Scott on Saturday, Haylee stopped by to see her mother. She had been meaning to go, and conveniently, it was on the way to her destination.

She parked in the short driveway in front of the one-car garage. The house was small and quaint, but cozy. It had only been she and her mom living in the house over the years and now Diane Jones spent her time there alone. She had people over now and again, but her mother had divorced Haylee's father and never remarried.

Snuggled into the suburbs, it was a quiet neighborhood, without much crime to claim. The house had the stereotypical white picket fence surrounding the yard, with yellow shutters and a pear tree out front with fruit that couldn't be picked fast enough. In the spring and summer, roses, pansies, and lilies lined the front of the home, presenting a picture-perfect landscaping. A meticulous gardener, Diane's hobby lent a serene quality to the atmosphere.

She used her key to let herself in, where she was greeted instantly by Peanut and Gizmo, her mom's Yorkshire terriers. Diane spoiled the two dogs, but it was easy for Haylee to see why. They were just so darn cute. She had grown attached to them herself before she moved out on her own and often missed them while she was away.

The scent of chocolate was noticeable as Haylee made her way to the small kitchen. Fresh baked goods were a common feature in the household, especially sweets. It was probably why Haylee enjoyed cooking herself.

Diane heard her daughter enter and had already risen from the kitchen table to give her a hug.

"Hi honey! Glad you could come by. I was just getting ready to take the cookies out of the oven. I'm watching Brian tonight."

Brian was her neighbor's lively four-year-old son. Diane

would watch him occasionally if his parents needed a night out to themselves.

"Are you?"

"Yep. It'll be a night of board games and Disney movies. What are your plans?" Diane pulled out a chair at the table for Haylee.

"Going to a friend's house." Haylee bent over in her chair to pet the two excited animals that had waited patiently for her attention. "I did buy some new furniture, and it was delivered earlier in the week. You'll have to come by to take a look."

"Of course I will." Diane smiled with pride at her daughter, constantly pleased she was doing so well. "By the way, I have a couple of boxes for you to take."

"I'm not surprised." Her mother anxiously unloaded Haylee's belongings that had been stored in the attic each time she came by. The boxes contained old pictures, books, even clothes that she wasn't quite sure what to do with. Currently, they were stacking up in the closet of her spare bedroom without having been opened.

The oven timer sounded off, and Diane rounded the corner to grab the batch of cookies.

"Do you want one?" she shouted to Haylee. "They're best warm, straight from the oven."

"Sure. One," Haylee insisted. "And I don't need to take any home with me to answer your next question."

Diane smirked, knowing that was most certainly the next thing she was going to ask. "Fine. Suit yourself. More for Brian and me."

Haylee was amazed her mom still had all her teeth in spite of her intense sweet tooth. The petite woman in front of her never encountered any problems from her sugar intake. Haylee, on the other hand, often wondered if it was possible for her to gain weight solely by looking at dessert.

Diane placed two plates on the table before she sat across from her daughter. Melted chocolate oozed from the side of the cookie in front of her. Four eyes stared intensely from a few feet away, but the dogs knew not to come closer to beg.

"What time are you supposed to be there tonight?"

"Ah, an hour or so. No rush."

"Are you going with Kathy?" Diane knew how close the women were. When they had been younger, Kathy was at her home so often that at times she felt as though she had two daughters.

Haylee broke her gooey treat in two before biting into the center. "No." She chewed slowly. "Scott."

Diane lifted an eyebrow. "Who's that?"

"Someone I just met. We went out last weekend. No big deal." As close as they were, some things Haylee thought best to omit from conversation with Mom—dating details in particular. Diane's wary, protective nature usually had her force-feeding advice to Haylee. What she didn't understand was that Haylee was wary enough herself.

"Well that's nice. You should bring him by sometime."

"Yeah, we'll see." Haylee gave her some credit for leaving it at that. She rose to take her empty plate to the kitchen sink. "Don't worry, I'm not planning on running off with him," she claimed sarcastically.

"Since I'm just now hearing about him, I would really hope not."

Haylee rolled her eyes to spite her mother. "Give me a little credit would ya?"

Diane's lips instinctively puckered. "It's not you that I don't trust."

Don't I know it, Haylee thought. "Stop fretting. Like I said, it's no big deal."

She grabbed her keys off the table, gave each dog a treat from the jar in the kitchen. "I gotta go."

She kissed her mother on the cheek before she went out the door. "Love ya."

"Love ya." Diane watched from the threshold as her daughter pulled the car out of the driveway. Haylee could say it hundreds of times, but she would still worry. It came with the territory.

Chapter 5

The sign on the front door said to make her way around the side of the house toward the backyard. Haylee could hear loud voices before she even rounded the corner.

She was empty-handed, but Scott had insisted that there was nothing she needed to bring. Overhead, it was cloudy, but the forecast promised no rain. Yet still, Haylee wore jeans and a sweatshirt to keep the chill from the wind out of her bones.

The grill had already been lit and Haylee could smell the charcoal burning when she pushed open the gate. Eyes fell upon her as she entered, some of them confused because they didn't recognize her. But they quickly went back to college football on the television that had been wheeled out onto the deck.

She was in fact fashionably late, and it appeared she was the last to arrive. A dozen or so people sat in folding chairs, some with a plate of food on their lap, others with just a cup in their hands. Hesitantly, she took a few steps forward and was glad when Scott emerged from the crowd.

"You made it," Scott smiled as he approached her.

"Sorry I'm a little late. I got caught up visiting my Mom."

"No worries, we're just getting started. Come on." He gently took a hold of her arm and led her toward the group. "Are you hungry?"

"Sure, yeah."

A card table had been set up buffet style in the kitchen. A large plate containing burgers and hot dogs from the grill, potato salad, chips, and baked beans were among its contents. Haylee was instructed to help herself, which she did, and Scott promptly disappeared to get her some soda from the garage.

When she stepped out of the sliding glass door back onto the deck, she was being gestured toward an empty chair. She sat, and the person motioning her over introduced himself as Sam, the host of the gathering.

"Nice house you have here," she told him. She had noticed the kitchen had been recently upgraded with new appliances and countertops. From there, the living area with its gleaming hardwood floors was visible. The green, manicured yard was a great size and was enclosed by a wooden privacy fence. The brick house had to be many years old, but didn't show it.

"I'll have to tell my landlord that. It's a rental." Sam lowered into a seat beside Haylee. "But thanks."

Sam introduced her to the other guests, and explained that most of them worked together. It was common for them to get together on Saturday or Sunday, or both, to watch football games during the season. Sometimes they even placed bets if their favorite teams were playing. On an occasion when there was evening game, it was expected that the fun would last well into the late hours, as was the case that night.

While Haylee listened to Sam and ate, she wondered what was keeping Scott. It had been more than a few minutes now that he had vanished. She was a little uncomfortable knowing she was the odd man out, the only newcomer. It would be helpful for Scott to be around to break the ice.

As if sensing her thoughts, he exited the house and set the cola beside her. By now, the small portions of food she had taken were gone, and she washed it down with half the soda in one gulp.

"I was starting to think you got lost there."

"Oh uh, I was stopped on the way out by Eric, he was telling me about a new girl he's seeing. He was rambling on so much, I didn't have the heart to interrupt. Too bad she had to work tonight."

"It is. It would have been nice to have an ally here, someone else new to the group. What does she do that has her working on Saturday night?"

Sam was called into the house, and Scott took his seat when he rose. "She works at a steakhouse downtown. I've been there, they have great food." Scott leaned in close enough that she went rigid. "Speaking of….," he trailed off.

He used his thumb to remove the tiniest bit of ketchup that had stuck to the corner of Haylee's mouth and then wiped it on his jeans. "You missed some," he told her.

Haylee felt the flush of embarrassment. Not necessarily for being sloppy, but because she could imagine the humor Sam had gotten out of it. She cleared her throat. "I can be a little messy. Guess you noticed that though."

"Only because I was looking closely at you." His dark eyes seemed to be looking very closely at her, scanning over every little pore in her face. "Otherwise, it wouldn't have been noticeable."

At least Sam probably wasn't having a laugh at her expense. But now there was a different problem—the knowledge of Scott's admission that he was studying her. She had seen him doing it on their last date as well. The worry of it was not that she was being scrutinized, but that she felt captivated by his gaze. It drew her in.

She broke eye contact. "That's good to know. I could have walked around all night like that without a clue. I'm sure someone would have spotted it eventually and then I could have been known as 'the ketchup girl' to your friends."

"Nah, by the time they all stop watching the game, the beer would have stumped their vision."

Haylee jumped when suddenly everyone yelled loudly, cheering. "Hmm, they are getting more rowdy. Maybe you're right."

"This is minor. You haven't seen anything yet."

On the next play, the home team scored and Haylee was able to see what he meant. Everyone was on their feet, arms in the air, cups being toasted around the circle. Had the view of the television not been blocked, she was certain the team that had made the touchdown was less boisterous than the group in front of her.

"Do you want to go inside? They'll only get louder."

Haylee shook head. "No. They're entertaining, like having a show within a show."

Before he could convince her it was a good idea to go inside and be alone, Sam returned and interrupted.

"Did you still want to fish tomorrow? Weather is supposed to be great. May be our last chance for awhile."

He had almost forgotten. "Of course, was planning on it."

Sam looked to Haylee. "You could join us if you'd like."

Scott opened his mouth to decline for Haylee but then shut it, taken aback when she spoke.

"Sounds like fun. I might," she glanced over to Scott. "If that's okay with you."

With his lips pursed and his eyebrows raised, he shrugged. "Fine with me."

"Great." As abruptly as he came, Sam wandered off again.

"Would I be intruding? I'm not even sure I can come, I have a lot I need to get done tomorrow."

"No. I'm just surprised that it sounds fun to you. Do you have a pole?"

"Well, no. Honestly, I've never been, but I haven't had a chance to try, either. I'm open to trying anything once." She stopped until another round of applauding subsided. "Plus, it's supposed to be a beautiful day."

Scott absently rubbed his chin. He was pleasantly surprised by her attitude. "I have extra gear. As long as you don't catch more than I do, the invitation stands."

"I don't think that will be a problem." Now that the sun had set, the air was cooler. Haylee folded her arms across her chest in an effort to keep warm. Even still, a shiver escaped her.

"C'mon, let's go inside and find a blanket for you."

Unable to resist the cold, she obliged. She excused herself to the restroom, and when she returned Scott was waiting on the couch. A fleece blanket was draped over his outstretched arms and invited Haylee to come inside. When she dropped in next to him, he folded each side around her and rubbed the sides of her arms to create more heat. She could smell the musky cologne that was sprayed on his shirt, and despite the ringing in her ears, thought she could hear the thump of her heartbeat.

She didn't have the guts to look over her shoulder, she knew how close his face was when she felt his breath on her neck. Instead, she wrapped herself tighter in the covers, and in one easy move slid to her right to lean against the armrest.

Light from the kitchen poured into the room, illuminating her surroundings. The recliner and love seat near her sat empty, proving the two of them were the only ones inside the house. From Scott's posture, Haylee could tell he had no intention upon going back outside, if only for the time being. His head was tilted, and was resting in the hand that was propped up on the top of the sofa. He sat quiet, as though waiting for her to say something.

She broke the ice and asked him questions, anything she could think of, ranging from work to hobbies. Scott obligingly answered and asked his own in return. The chatter helped distract Haylee from feeling tense.

He maintained his distance, sitting relaxed beside her. More than once, Haylee caught herself picking at her fingernails under the covers, a nervous habit. It took a lot of willpower to not start chewing on them.

Eventually, others trickled in the house, unable to stand the falling temperature outdoors. The silence they had enjoyed was now replaced by loud conversation. Haylee snuck a peek at her watch to discover they had been talking for over an hour.

Warm now, she shed the blanket engulfing her. "I better get going. It's getting late."

Scott took the blanket she had folded and threw it over the back of the couch. "Are you sure? If you were entertained before, you surely will be now. I overheard someone saying we won."

A puff of air escaped her as part sigh, part laugh. "I'm sure I would be. Maybe next time."

Haylee said good-bye to everyone with a wave as Scott announced her departure. She thanked Sam for having her, and Sam reminded her about the next day. She said she'd try to make it.

Scott trailed on her heels out onto the porch.

"Where did you park?" he asked.

Cars lined the street as they had when she arrived. Haylee dug for the keys that had made their way to the bottom of her purse, fumbled with them when she finally pulled them out.

"I'm about a block down." She descended a step as she said it.

He followed. "Let me walk you there. The streetlamps aren't helping much."

He was right. Her vehicle wasn't even visible from where she stood. But she was suddenly intent upon evading him.

"Don't worry about it. I'll walk fast, it's not far away."

Before she could scurry off, Scott clutched her hand and pulled her in toward him. Her pulse quickened, and she felt her stomach tie in a knot. As he leaned in, her breath caught, but she released it in a wheeze when he merely kissed her cheek, then let go of her hand.

"Good night."

She felt the tension in her muscles ebb, and allowed the corner of her mouth to curve upward.

"Good night," she resounded back. "I'll call if I can join you tomorrow."

When she reached the sidewalk, she glanced over her shoulder to see Scott still standing on the stoop. She shifted her purse so that it fit snugly under her arm, and quickened her pace. The tall oak trees lining the walkway blocked most of the artificial light so that Haylee was surrounded by shadows. She let out a quiet greeting when she passed a young woman who was making her way from her house to her car at the curb. She was already pulling out into the street when Haylee finally reached her car.

She waited until the car had passed, then curved around into the street while she pressed 'unlock' on her keyless remote.

Haylee heard the crackle of a snapped branch behind her, and whirling around, she was instantly faced with an unfamiliar man in black who promptly revealed the silver gleam of his pocketknife to her.

"Don't scream," were the first words he said to her in his deep voice.

She didn't dare, the blade was mere inches from her throat. Though her vision was hindered by the night, it was obvious the person in front of her was twice her size. The baseball cap on his head was pulled low, further shielding his face from view. The only detail she could make out was the short facial hair lining his jaw.

"Give me your purse." Haylee could smell the alcohol on his breath as he barked out the order to her. His hand looked like a catcher's mitt as he reached for Haylee's shoulder to give her a shove. "Turn around."

She let out a whimper as she obeyed. She wished she could yell for Scott, but wondered if he was even still out on the porch. Branches blocked her view of Sam's stoop.

Panic surged through her like an electric current in her blood. She felt frozen in place as her mind raced over a hundred frightening thoughts. As her bag slipped down her arm, she prayed he would take the damn thing and leave. She couldn't care less about the contents at this point.

He didn't comply. Haylee was nauseous as his free hand slid down the side of her body. She gripped her keys tightly, forcing herself to overcome the fear. Despite the lack of preparation for this type of situation, she knew she needed to focus her wits if she wanted to get away safely.

The man could sense her frailty, in comparison to his strength. And she could sense his intentions of overpowering her.

His grubby fingers glided up her shirt, on bare skin. She instinctively shuddered in disgust and she tried to back away from his touch, but he had her pinned against the car from behind. With the knife's sharp edge still at her throat, there was no retreat.

She was already aware of the onset of bruising from the pressure of his elbow in her back. The pain somehow subsided when his lips brushed against the curve of her neck, her concentration back on resistance. With his focus now on touching her, the hand that held the blade was slipping away from her. She writhed against him, to no avail.

In one swift motion, the man opened the rear door of her car and simultaneously thrust her inside. Haylee landed with a thud, face-first on the seat, and had the metallic taste of blood on her tongue as she rolled herself over.

Haylee had one advantage. Her attacker was clumsy from his intoxicated state. His weapon had slipped from his fingers while pushing her down, and he was either unaware or unconcerned by it. She swallowed her terror, along with the blood from the lip she bit when she fell, and posed herself to fight.

Chapter 6

Scott made his way back in the house after he saw the car maneuver down the street. He had been tempted to follow her there, for more reasons than one, despite her stubborn refusals. His concerned had mounted when he lost sight of her, but he had relaxed when he heard the roar of her engine and had seen her headlights flicker on.

Inside, everyone was carrying on as they had been. When Sam caught sight of Scott, he waved him over.

"Hey, you've been nominated to go to the store. We need another case of beer. I wasn't expecting so many people."

Sam lifted Scott's hand, slapping money into it. "Why me?"

"Because I know you've had way less than anyone else here. Plus, you might want to buy something for tomorrow. Fishing isn't as fun without the brew."

Scott exhaled audibly. "I'll be right back."

Scott plucked one of Sam's jackets out of the coat closet before heading back out the door, heading in the same direction Haylee had walked just moments ago.

As her assailant bent to enter the vehicle, Haylee braced herself, grabbing the passenger seat for leverage, and kicked him hard in the stomach. He stumbled backward, grunting from the pain, and was hunched over clutching where Haylee had made impact. She took the opportunity to scream while she frantically reached for the door to shut it.

The pause in battle was brief, and the stranger recovered quickly from Haylee's assault. She berated herself for not doing more damage, thinking she should have kicked his face. She promptly believed herself capable of serious violence, and wished she had a weapon in hand. But she had nothing, and the man was able to catch the door before Haylee could slam it shut.

She struggled against it, audibly, and was both shocked and relieved when he abruptly released the door and ran away.

She was dizzy with emotion, and her terror returned when a man once again flashed in front of her face. Her alarm faded when she steadied herself enough to realize Scott now knelt beside her.

Panting, her breath came out in jagged gasps, and she was visibly shaking. Scott gripped her wrist, trying to get her attention.

"Holy shit! Are you alright?" He seemed to be shouting it at her.

Her gaze darted back and forth over the street. She couldn't yet believe that it was over.

When she finally stopped searching, Scott's question registered in her mind. The floodgate opened then, with tears streaming down unintentionally. "Yes. Fine......,"she caught the glimmer of metal on the ground out of the corner of her eye. "No...No I'm not," she sobbed.

He brushed her hair back behind her ears. "It's okay. I scared him off. I would've kicked his ass if I could have gotten my hands on him."

Helping her up, practically carrying her, he said, "C'mon let's get you inside where it's safe." He lifted her chin. "We'll calm you down and get you cleaned up."

He shuffled her back to one of the bedrooms. Gasps and whispers went through the crowd as they glimpsed Haylee's pale skin, rumpled clothes, and tear-stained cheeks. Behind her, Scott waved people off as they stepped forward to ask questions.

With the door shut behind them, Haylee plopped down on a chair and wiped her damp face. Her heart was still pounding in her chest, but she was slowly composing herself. It helped to keep thinking how she had come out in one piece, and the frightening scenarios that she had been sure were likely to happen had not been realized. She had been lucky. Lucky that Scott had shown up when he did.

She needed to occupy herself. "Is there a phone I can use? Mine was in my purse, which he scurried off with. The sooner I can get all my accounts cancelled, the better."

Scott dug in his pocket. "Sure. Use mine." He handed it to her.

Haylee pointed to the computer tucked in the corner. "Is that connected to the Internet? I'll have to look up the eight-hundred numbers I need to call."

He jumped in front of her. "Yeah let me just….," he trailed off. He took hold of the mouse for a few seconds in a frenzy. "There. Have at it."

She settled in front of the monitor before grabbing a pen and a sheet of scrap paper off the desk. Scott clutched the door knob, asking before he left, "Do you need anything else?"

Haylee looked at the list she had just made, noting how

sloppy her handwriting was from the tremors in her hand. "I could use a drink." She added, "Anything."

While Haylee made her calls, Scott hastily answered the questions he was bombarded with the instant he walked into the kitchen. He refused offers of help, saying he had everything under control, and assured them all that Haylee was alright. He mixed her a rum and coke, more rum than coke, then slipped quietly back through the bedroom door.

Haylee was ending a call as he walked up behind her. He set the cocktail on the desk.

"Don't get too carried away," he said, pointing at the glass. "You'll want to make a police report before the night is over, and it won't be a good thing if you're sloshed."

She lifted the cup to her lips, taking a big swallow anyway. "I'm so worked up that I'm not sure it'll do much except sooth my nerves a little." She drank again, this time only taking a sip. "But I'll keep that in mind."

He nodded. "When you're finished, I'll drive you to the police station, or we can have an officer meet us at your house if that's easier. That way, you don't have everyone here butting in."

"Alright. One more call, and I'll be done."

When the officer finally left her house, it was nearly one in the morning. She had done all she could for the time being, and was thoroughly exhausted. However, she wasn't sure she would be able to sleep.

She had been reminded that her current address was on her stolen driver's license, and now she feared her attacker would show up at her home. Scott tried to convince her that it was unlikely, but nevertheless, she wanted to take as many precautions as possible.

"Would you mind staying at my place tonight? I um, I'd

rather not be alone until I can install some kind of security system. It's a little late to ask someone else."

He was going to suggest it, had she not. "I can do that."

"Thanks. And if I haven't said it, thank you for you've done tonight. I don't know what might have happened had you not come along to my rescue."

"It's a good thing I came back out. I thought I had seen your car pull away."

"No. That was one of the neighbors. She left right before I got to my car."

"Oh. Well, try not to think of the alternatives. You'll drive yourself crazy."

She involuntarily shuddered. "Right." She spun on her heel in the direction of the hallway. "I have an air mattress that you can sleep on, and I'll sleep on the couch, if that works." She was not only spooked but paranoid, and her bed seemed miles from where Scott would be. There wasn't any point in him being there if he wouldn't even hear if something happened to her.

It wouldn't be his preference, but technically it would *work*. "Sure."

"Let me grab some blankets."

Haylee returned with enough linen for the both of them and Scott moved the coffee table before inflating his makeshift bed. Before she settled in, Haylee checked the doors and windows to make sure they were all securely locked.

"All good?" Scott asked when she returned.

"It looks that way."

Scott was already perched upon the air mattress with blankets pulled up under his arms. He looked calm, not at all worried like Haylee. He was succeeding in comforting her, and she had liked how it felt having him there for her.

It had consoled her to have someone to share the burden with.

She had gravitated to him and she decided to go with it before she could rethink it.

Instead of hopping on the couch, Haylee knelt beside Scott and eased herself down beside him. She perched one hand on his cheek, turning his head gently, before pressing her lips to his.

She lingered there a moment, letting herself enjoy the soft contact before pulling away.

Neither of them said anything, only pierced each other with their eyes. When she began to rise, Scott tugged her arm, sending her back down to him. When he kissed her, he was slightly more insistent. The fingers of one hand ran through her hair while the other glided down her back. She briefly lay helpless across his chest until their mouths parted, then she slowly lifted herself up and backed away.

"Good night."

He only watched as Haylee rested her head on the pillow pushed up against the sofa cushions, before she rolled onto her side so that her back was turned to him.

He *had* been ready to fall asleep before she had surprisingly stirred him. Scott stared at the ceiling, willing away his arousal. He folded his hands tightly over his stomach while blowing the air out of his lungs.

Even with all the stress in the last few hours, Haylee fell asleep fast. But her dreams were disturbed, replaced by nightmares. She first awoke after reliving the horror from earlier. Sitting up suddenly, thinking it had happened all over again, she hugged herself while the cold sweat made her shiver. Listening, there wasn't a sound in the house, except her pounding heart and labored breathing…and Scott's snoring.

Despite her anxiety, Haylee snickered as she listened to

Scott. A whole marching band might not have been able to wake him. He was out like a light, in obvious need of slumber. The television remote was inches from her, and she thought about sending it crashing to the floor to see if he would react. She doubted it. Some gate keeper she thought, but chuckled as she lowered herself back to the pillow.

Chapter 7

The storm was raging outside with the sound of forceful rain on the rooftop. Trees were blowing up against the window as thunder was rumbling up in the heavens. The racket awoke Haylee from her sleep but she was delighted when she saw the clock only read three thirty in the morning. She still had a few hours before the alarm would go off to signal it was time to get up. She pulled the covers up to her nose, smiling while listening to the downpour, pleased to be in her warm bed.

She closed her eyes and almost drifted back to sleep until she heard angry voices down the hall. Although her parents were doing their best to keep the volume at a minimum, their fury and frustration was not allowing them to do so. Shocked, Haylee listened to her parents argue for the first time. She was unaware of the fact that these fights occurred regularly, only out of her earshot.

The wind and thunder became louder just then, and the actual content of the argument could not be heard. Tears of panic came to her eyes because she wished she could hear the dispute. Surely it was something minor.

But what were they doing up this late? A door slammed and then Haylee clearly heard her father say he was leaving. To go where? Maybe he had to leave for a work trip at the last minute and her mom was just upset about that. He had to travel often so she concluded that had to be the issue.

Daring to peek through the bedroom door she cracked open, suitcases immediately came into view. I was right, she thought. Haylee started to turn to go back to bed until her parents both came out into the hallway. Her Mom was crying and pointing her finger in her Dad's face. He had his hands up in the air and for a split second Haylee thought he was going to strike her. Instead, he gripped her by the shoulders, giving her a shove backward before he scooped up his suitcases and disappeared out of sight.

Though she lay back in bed worried, she somehow was able to convince herself everything was alright.

When she stumbled downstairs in the morning, still heavy from sleep, breakfast was served as usual. But her mother looked troubled and tired. Diane managed a smile for her daughter, wondering if she was the only one who knew it was fake.

Haylee stared blankly at her when she sat down to eat her eggs. She wanted to know for certain what was going on.

"Mom, did Dad have to go on a trip?"

Diane pondered the question for a moment. She was positive that last night's fight was the couple's last. After Ken had left, she had spent the rest of the night trying to figure out what to say to Haylee, and in the end she had decided it would be best to tell her the truth.

"No honey he didn't. He is going to be living somewhere

else now. But he still loves you and you will go to see him."

Diane didn't want to believe that she wouldn't be the only one that Ken no longer wanted to speak to. He had changed so much in the last year that she couldn't be certain he felt any responsibility to his family and his 'old life' as he had put it. It wasn't something she was prepared to discuss with Haylee.

"But why? I don't understand. He doesn't want to live with us anymore?"

Diane had already shed her share of tears and thought there weren't anymore left. When she saw Haylee's eyes well up, she knew she had been wrong.

She somehow fought back her misery.

"I'm sorry Haylee. It's not at all your fault." She bent down, kissed Haylee's forehead before giving her a hug. "Please don't cry. Everything will be alright."

Her mother lifted her chin so that their eyes met. "I promise."

Haylee nodded slowly.

"Would you rather not go to school today?"

Haylee wiped her face with the tissue that had been handed to her. "No. I'll be okay."

This time when Haylee awoke, it was morning. And she was relieved because she couldn't handle another nightmare.

With her father's hasty exit fresh on her mind, she tiptoed to her bathroom for a shower. Scott was still fast asleep when she passed him. Haylee tried to forget her dreams and the anguish associated with them. The memory was so vivid despite taking place years ago. Talk about waking up on the wrong side of the bed.

The hot spray of water felt good on her body as she stood

under the nozzle. When she washed her hair, she rubbed her temples in the hopes of dispelling a forthcoming headache. As the steam built up around her, she could feel her muscles go limp in relaxation.

By the time she finished, she felt refreshed. She threw on jeans and a T-shirt before walking out into the living room. Scott was nowhere to be found. She was offended that he left without a good-bye. Maybe he hadn't wanted to stay there as much as she thought. He hadn't even bothered to deflate the mattress or fold a blanket.

Before her irritation could increase, the front door glided open by Scott's hand. He coughed and cleared his throat, shutting the door quietly behind him prior to noticing Haylee standing there. He jumped ever so slightly.

"Morning."

She sulked to herself, both for believing him to be so rude and for getting so upset that he had vanished.

"I thought you had left for a second there."

Scott ran the cigarette butt under the faucet before throwing it in the trash. "Nope. Don't have anywhere to be just yet." He winked at her. "How did you sleep?"

"Decent. Could have been worse." She snatched up blankets to put away. "I'd ask you, but I think I already know the answer. I woke up at one point and you were sound asleep."

"That doesn't surprise me. Not much gets in the way of my rest."

Scott drug the coffee table back to its place after Haylee had cleaned up, then plucked his car keys off the floor.

"Are you hungry?" she asked. She was uncomfortable, and didn't know what else to say.

"No, I'll get something later. Sam is on his way to pick me up for our fishing outing." Scott had driven Haylee's car to her house the night before, and had left his parked in front of Sam's.

"Oh. Right. Have fun," she told him.

"You're not going to join us?"

She shrugged. "No. I'm going to look into getting my locks changed today. I'd rather get that done sooner than later."

"That's a good idea. Will you be okay here by yourself?"

"Should be. I'd like to think the immediate danger is over."

Scott tied his shoe laces since he hadn't bothered to before. "You'll be fine," he assured her.

He stepped over to hug her before walking out the door. "I'll talk to you soon."

Chapter 8

The next month went by quickly. Haylee was busy, mainly with work. Several transactions had been negotiated in a short time, all with closing dates clustered together. Everyone wanted to move before snow hit the ground.

The closings she attended, along with the money they garnered, helped to alleviate her tension. Not only was it a bonus to have extra money before the holiday season, but she had experienced a lull since her last paycheck. It was one downfall of the business she was in—it was feast or famine. At times the money rolled in, but there were also dry spells where her savings dwindled and thoughts of classified ad perusals crossed her mind.

Haylee stuck to a tight budget for instances when these famines occurred so that she could stretch her finances until another sale was completed, but at times it was hard not to panic. The mortgage due date would loom over her head, taunting her with its deadline during the months she had income shortages. Luckily she had been able to manage her money well thus far to avoid any problems.

Keeping her clients happy was a full-time job itself. She received calls at all hours of the day, nights and weekends, even holidays. She knew she was too accommodating, doing what was asked of her even when it was an inconvenience. She wanted to set stricter limits on her availability, but somehow she always failed to stick to that goal.

On the other hand, she did like to keep busy, so being accessible gave her plenty to do. When her phone rang steadily, she felt needed, like her time was in high demand. Unlike her finances, she hadn't found the balance for her schedule.

Her on-the-go lifestyle would surely be less appealing eventually. The constant demands and needs of clientele would have to take a back burner if she ever hoped to have a family. It was her belief that if she worked hard now, it would pay off in the future. Her career would run on a referral basis, not on her chasing down the leads. She longed for the day when repeat business fell onto her doorstep without her constantly having to churn up interest.

When she was free, she had seen Scott several times. He hadn't always been available when she proposed they get together, but they had found time to spend with each other amidst their busy schedules.

Her thoughts centered around him often. He had managed to break through her invisible barrier and was penetrating her heart. The qualities she liked most in him were the exact ones she lacked, and she believed they complemented each other well. For once, she could envision future experiences with a man that were special, committed.

Tonight, was one of those special occasions. Scott had invited her to his company's Christmas party, albeit the last minute because he had forgotten about it. It was actually quite the lavish event. T&M Incorporated didn't skimp when it came to the employee's holiday celebration. It helped that the president of the corporation, Logan Black, was a big fan of the season and therefore passed the love on to the staff.

A ballroom was rented at a local hotel, and the attire for the night was formal at Mr. Black's behest. Men were to wear jackets and ties while ladies pulled their best dresses from the closet. It so happened that Haylee didn't have anything to pull from *her* closet, so she was headed to the mall.

She was short on time, so she strode into one department store determined to find something, anything that could work. As she began to sift through the racks, her eyes bulged when she flipped over price tags. Her selection was being narrowed instantly, based solely on cost. It wasn't feasible to spend much when the dress would sit in the back of her closet collecting dust until she had the chance, if any, to wear it again.

She had considered borrowing one, but had no luck there. Most of her friends, like her, hadn't any need for formal wear, and the ones that did were a different size than her.

A clearance rack was tucked in the corner with items jammed on its rail. Haylee squeezed past a small group of women, walking sideways so that she didn't knock down garment hangers from their perches, and found the section with her size.

There weren't many options, yet she managed to find one that appealed to her. It was floor length, and a dark navy blue satin. Spaghetti straps connected to a bodice that featured a velvet fabric around the bust. A matching shawl was included for colder weather. The tag on the side revealed that it was half off, well within her budget.

She let herself in the dressing room and hastily changed.

The frock was a little snug in the chest, but she could deal with that. It flared ever so slightly below the waist, masking her hips nicely. Once she put on shoes that had a heel, the bottom hem would be the perfect distance from the floor. She silently relished her acquisition, knowing full well clothing shopping was never that easy.

Pleased with her find, she was on her way home in no time.

Her friend Wendy was due at her house in half an hour. Wendy worked in a nearby salon as a hairdresser and insisted that she come by to help Haylee get ready. Without fail, Wendy looked like she had stepped out of a magazine ad. She had a talent for not only making herself look great, but others, too. In addition to her job, she was taking classes on fashion design, her proclaimed true passion.

Wendy arrived with a small case with her 'tools' inside. She was quick to rant on about school, how hard it was to make sure she attended classes, and the work it required. If you let her, Wendy could talk your ear off. Haylee had to butt in a few times just to get a word in edgewise.

She worked quickly since Haylee hadn't allotted her much time. Wendy had to swat Haylee's hand away every now and then when Haylee started to interfere. The look Wendy was giving her was simple and in no need of her friend's meddling.

Carefully pinning the last stray hairs in place, Wendy gave Haylee's hair a long douse of hairspray, then bent down in front of her to study her finished work. Satisfied, she parked herself in a chair and let out a long sigh as though she had just finished a marathon.

"Walah!" she said, "and there you have it."

The mirror reflected the mass of curls that were pinned loosely at the nape of Haylee's neck. A few free tresses framed Haylee's face.

"Thanks, I appreciate you doing this. I'm glad you volunteered to come, not just for the help but because I haven't seen you lately."

Plucking a strand of Haylee's hair off her shirt, she said, "I know! Get you a boyfriend and you fall off the face of the earth." She threw one leg over the other, the four-inch heel of her shoe hanging from her foot like a dagger. "It's okay though, I understand."

Haylee's eyes fell to the floor. "Have I been that bad?"

Wendy waved her hand in the air to brush off the question. "Really, it's fine. Just miss ya is all. You seem happy, so that's all that matters."

Meeting Wendy's eyes, she smiled. It was hard to hold back her bliss. "I am. It's sort of been all encompassing. I haven't been able to think of much else."

Wendy nodded in agreement. "Been there. Makes me a little envious you know. My list of single friends is steadily decreasing, and soon I am going to end up all alone."

Haylee rumpled her face to show her disparity. "Get out. You know you'll find someone soon enough."

Sighing, she replied, "I suppose. Doesn't feel that way right now though."

"Take it for what it's worth and just have fun. In the meantime, I'll see if Scott has any friends I can match you up with."

That helped her outlook. "Alright, but only if I get to go to fancy parties too," she joked.

Haylee snickered. "It is a company Christmas party. It's not like this happens any other time."

Haylee spent as much time as she could with Wendy before she left to pick up Scott. She had reluctantly agreed to drive them. Driving in a dress and heels was not the most comfortable undertaking. Maybe she could get him to drive her car when she got there.

Scott was waiting outside for her, slightly irritated that she was a few minutes late. He didn't want to be one of the last guests walking in. He bit his lip, knowing full well that he wouldn't be able to let it go.

She was cheery when he climbed in, but he didn't think twice about dampening her mood.

"Running a little behind?" he asked with a snarl.

Haylee was taken aback. "Oh, um…I guess a little. Sorry. I didn't realize we were on a strict timetable."

He brushed it off the best he could. "Whatever. Let's just get there."

She felt slighted, but was determined not to let it bother her. She pasted on a grin and proceeded to change the subject.

"You look great."

He tugged on his tie, loosening his collar some. He couldn't exactly argue. A suit had a way of doing for him what styled hair and cosmetics must do for the ladies. He felt important, composed, confidant. His attire intensified his daily attitude.

"Thanks. You look pretty good yourself." His eyes wandered over Haylee's body from head to toe. While she drove, the slit in her dress exposed her leg, teasing Scott's senses. He brushed a loose curl of hair off Haylee's neck, sending a tremble down her spine.

Haylee tossed her head to the side and batted her eyelashes at him. "Do I?"

"Yeah. I have to be honest though. I would have liked to see more skin."

Haylee furrowed her brow and turned to see Scott's eyebrows raised provocatively.

"Oh come on, I am messing with you."

"Better be. Besides, I wouldn't have wanted you to get

jealous if I had chosen something racier. All eyes would have been on me," she said matter-of-factly.

"They already will be," he told her.

"Well lucky for you, I'll be on your arm." She winked at him. "Just yours," she added when she reached for his hand.

He knew it to be true.

Scott's worry proved to be unfounded when they arrived. They had made good time driving there, and plenty of people were busy parking their cars in the lot. They followed a group in through the front door.

The lobby was warm and welcoming, and a sign had been displayed that pointed in the direction they were to go. A table was set up down the hall, and Scott quickly collected their name tags before entering.

The rented space looked as though it had been set up carefully, and the decorations were hardly sparse. White lights were strung from the ceiling, entwined with garland in honor of the holiday. Each table included a vase of poinsettias and the crisp fresh scent traveled through the room. Wreaths of pine were hung on the walls, and there was even an ornamented tree with a bright gold star on top. Christmas had erupted all over the four walls, ceiling, and everywhere in between.

The crowd was a sea of black suits and long flowing frocks, most attendees with a plate of hors d'oeuvres in their hands, others with only cocktails. No one so much as glanced their way when they strode in. Scott scanned the mass of people and was able to find co-workers he regularly talked to. He pulled Haylee in that direction.

Scott was a flood of words right off the bat. Haylee had met most of the guys that stood in their huddle, but was uncharacteristically shy and quiet while she stood at Scott's side. She did her best to contribute to conversation when she could.

She waited patiently until Scott suggested they head to their table.

The task took longer than expected since Scott stopped to talk to everyone that came across their path. His company was much larger than she had realized. It was obvious to her that Scott was taking this opportunity to network. A few times Haylee had to discretely nudge him to remind him to introduce her.

Dinner was served family style, with large plates of food placed on the tables. They contained everything from sautéed vegetables to creamy pastas to tender meats. The portions were huge and everyone was more than able to get their fair share.

The award ceremony bored her since she didn't know any of the people being honored or what they had accomplished in order to be up on the stage. She resisted the urge to pull out her cell phone to play a game. Instead, she sat up straight, faked her interest, clapped when appropriate.

She also casually studied the expressions of others around her. Some appeared as bored as she. Others exuded disappointment, some admiration, and some Haylee suspected didn't agree with the associates' names that were being called. She could understand that much, she had felt the same way when she missed out on a sales award. At one point Scott leaned over to declare his intention of winning next year. Everything, he had asserted when probed.

Haylee was relieved the whole process didn't last long and that the band was playing before she knew it. She made a bee-line for the restroom, apparently having the same idea of many other women. The line was long by the time Haylee reached it.

She took a moment to glance in the mirror and to

freshen the red lipstick that had worn off her lips. Her ears perked when she heard Scott's name come out of a woman's mouth that had walked in the door. Taking her time, she listened as she blotted at a lipstick smudge with her finger, but the conversation was over. She blew it off, figuring there must be several men named Scott out in that room.

She snuck out to the lobby to quickly return a phone call. Her client called to confirm a walk-through for the house he was purchasing that they had scheduled for the next day. Haylee returned mere minutes later, surprised to see the woman from the bathroom standing with *her* Scott.

Haylee's sudden pang of jealousy was not only unfamiliar, but unwanted. And most likely, unwarranted.

Scott gave her a casual smile when she approached. "Haylee, this is Susan, one of my supervisors."

Simultaneously, both women said, "Nice to meet you."

"We were talking about some of the company's new policies. Susan, if you'll excuse me….," he trailed off as he turned to Haylee.

"Of course. I'll catch you later."

At that, she gave a little smirk before walking away. Haylee felt as if she had disrupted them. The pair dispersed as soon as she came up.

"I didn't mean to interrupt."

He shrugged. "We were done anyway. We see eye to eye on a lot of things having to do with work, so we like to bitch about it to one another."

Haylee watched Susan saunter up to another male associate. "It's good to vent sometimes."

Scott slipped his arm around her torso, turning her to face him in the process.

"How's your feet?" she asked him.

"My feet?" he responded quizzically.

"Yeah, as in do you have two left ones? Or can I talk you into a dance?"

Couples were scattered in front of the band, clutching each other while they spun in circles. Sarcasm dripped from every syllable when he told her, "Sounds great."

Once intermingled with the other duos, Haylee placed her arms tightly around Scott's neck as she began to sway with the music. She leaned in close to him, breathing in the scent of his cologne. It was a blend of musk, spice, and woods—and all purely masculine.

Scott's fingers glided around Haylee's waist, tactfully stopping short of going any lower. The sight of her had him going wild inside. She almost looked like a different person with the dress and the way her hair was. The garment she had chosen loosely clung to her body, leaving just the right amount to imagination. The slit on the side of it teasingly went up her left leg but stopped short when it reached the knee. He couldn't help but wonder what was underneath the view.

The slow rhythmic steps put Haylee in a daze. They had a calming effect that had her sinking into Scott's embrace. For a moment, she forgot she was in the middle of a crowded room.

"I love you." She was entranced enough that she let those little words slip out. Immediately, she wanted to take them back, wishing there was some kind of rewind button she could hit. But it was too late.

She thought it was true. She *had* wanted to give it more time before bringing it up so that she could be sure, but the confession had prematurely come out.

It had given Scott a mild shock. Perhaps deep down he had seen it coming, but he still was not prepared for it. Looking at her pale face, he could tell she was self-conscious. Her expression pleaded with him not to smash her feelings.

"Love you too."

Scott saw it as a simple declaration of emotion, a name they were giving to the fondness they had for one another.

It was Haylee's turn to be taken aback. She had expected something along the lines of 'slow down, we hardly know each other'. Instead he had responded as she hoped he would.

A slow grin spread across her face before she briefly met his lips.

When Scott suggested he come to Haylee's house after the party, she was pretty sure how the rest of the night would unfold. And she had to admit, she was nervous.

She had eluded the situation thus far. If Scott had ever been frustrated with her about it, he hadn't shown any signs of it. She had maintained a distance with him, physically, and she hadn't even been sure why.

It was easier to remember now. For one, she wouldn't know what she was doing. The basics, yes of course she knew. But not the fine details that came with the experience.

Scott coolly ran one hand up Haylee's exposed thigh, from the seat next to her. Since the playing field was not even, Haylee thought it might be best to divulge that information. If he couldn't share her apprehensions, at least maybe he could be sympathetic to them.

After they had finally made it in her house, Scott sat close to her on the sofa, and she admitted her secret.

"You know, um….this is all new to me."

Scott's head was swimming from exhaustion. "Hmm, what's new to you?"

She had hoped he would catch on right away, but no

such luck. She decided to skip over the novel love aspects and get to the point.

"Sex," she blurted. It was awkward to acknowledge. She continued, "I'm making assumptions here, but my guess was that you didn't come to just snuggle."

The fog lifted some. It had been on his mind periodically through the night, and he would be lying if he said he didn't want the evening to end with it. What he hadn't anticipated was talking about it first, along with Haylee's disclosure.

He answered carefully. "I see. If you're not ready…."

"It's not that," she cut him off. "I, I more just wanted you to know so, in case you had to…guide me a little."

Scott sighed silently with some relief. He hadn't been quite sure what he was going to say next if she hadn't interrupted.

"Point taken. Don't worry about it," he told her as he pulled her closer, kissing her. She now laid with her body pressed atop his, Scott's hands sliding up her back. He found the zipper on the dress, pulled it down. "We'll take it slow."

Chapter 9

The sunlight piercing through the blinds roused Haylee from sleep, and her unclothed body was wedged against Scott's. Despite the slumber, her mind was still reeling from the night before. Her heart raced just thinking about it. Scott had eased her tension and she had felt comfortable in his embrace.

Haylee slipped on pants and a sweatshirt, paused at the door a moment to watch Scott sleep, then shut the door behind her.

She had plenty to do today. Her dinner guests would not arrive until later that evening, but she still needed to clean her house, grocery shop, and cook before they got there. Very uncharacteristic of her, she awoke with the energy to get moving right away.

From under the sink, Haylee grabbed the supplies she would need. Cloth in hand, she wiped tables, wondering how dust collected so fast. It felt like she had *just* cleaned them, but it probably had been much longer than she thought. She found household chores tedious, which didn't help with the frequency with which she would do them. Her home would never be one of those spotless types.

When Scott emerged, Haylee was battling with the broom and dustpan, bent over the kitchen floor.

With his hair awry and clothes disheveled, he approached the spot where Haylee was crouched down. "I need to take off. Would you run me over to my place before you get too involved there?"

Haylee rose and brushed her hands together. "Yeah. I just need to put on my shoes."

She stepped into her boots and snatched the car keys off her dining room table. "Don't forget about dinner tonight," she reminded him, even though she couldn't see how he could possibly forget. She had been sure to bring it up more than once. "At six," she added.

Scott nodded. "Game should be done in plenty of time."

"Game?"

"Uh-huh, I'm going over to Sam's at three for the basketball game."

Frustration was bubbling inside her. Not only because she knew she had made the plans for tonight clear, but because he was being short with her.

"I'd appreciate it if you came on time."

Scott shut the passenger side car door with a little more force than necessary. "I'll be here. Don't worry."

While she was out, Haylee picked up the groceries she needed. She somehow turned the doorknob with her arms full of paper bags, refusing to make more than one trip from the car.

With her goods put away, she finished tidying up. She vacuumed the carpet, loaded the dishwasher, and threw in some laundry. It took longer than she expected, but she figured she still had enough time to take a jog and shower before she needed to get started on dinner. The December air was a mild fifty degrees, and she wanted to take advantage of it.

An hour and a half later, she was back in her kitchen. She stuck a pair of headphones in her ears before she started dicing the onions and garlic she needed for her lasagna. Music was soon blaring for only her to hear.

It would just be six of them. Kathy was bringing Jake, and Scott invited his friend Tom so that it would be an even number for Wendy. Kathy said she would have wine in tow, so Wendy offered to tackle dessert. All Haylee had to worry about was everything else in between.

But she didn't care. Actually, dinner would be quite easy. She had made her baked lasagna, with both béchamel and marinara sauces, many times. It had crossed her mind to go so far as to make homemade noodles, but with everything she had to do, it only seemed like an extra hassle.

A caprese salad with ripe tomatoes and fresh mozzarella was also on the menu. With the prep work already finished for it, she would put the salad together at the last minute before everyone arrived.

Lost in her work, Haylee sang along with the music. Her head bobbed to the melodies, and her notes were out of key, but it didn't matter. No one was there to see it.

Or so she thought.

He was standing there behind her, watching, and didn't immediately make his presence known. It was entertaining to listen to her belt out familiar tunes. Her ponytail swayed as her body moved back and forth. Splashed on her cheek, he could detect the smallest bit of tomato sauce when her face turned to the side. Pots cluttered the stove, while bowls and ingredients accompanied the countertops. The whole scene was strangely arousing.

Haylee paused when she had the feeling someone was there. She eyed the knife that she had used to cut the vegetables before she had the urge to turn around.

She spun on him, arms flailing through the air, and she steadily screamed profanities when she realized there was no danger.

"What…the…hell!" It almost came out as a stutter.

Unable to hold it any louder, Scott's howl of laughter rang through the kitchen.

"Surprise," was his simple response.

"What are you doing here and how did you get in?"

"It's not hard to walk through the front door when it isn't locked."

Crap. Had she forgot to do that again? She was so focused on getting the groceries in that she obviously forgot to go back and lock the door. She had meant to be better about remembering to do that, knowing some stranger out there had her address.

"I had knocked, but apparently you didn't hear it, and now I see why. I knew you'd be here, so I tried the knob," he professed. "And I had been wrong. The game started at one so I came straight here when it was over."

"Oh. I wasn't expecting you."

"I can see that." She looked as though she was going to pounce on him.

"You scared the shit out of me. I'm still paranoid that asshole who stole my purse is going to show up here."

Seeing how she had turned white made him feel guilty. "He won't." He pulled her closer to him, embraced her. "I didn't mean to scare you."

She let out a long breath. "Forgiven." She pulled away from him, smoothing out the front of her shirt in the process. "I'd ask you to help, but everything is done at the moment."

"Probably best. I'm not very handy in the kitchen."

He closed the distance she had put between them, a conniving expression lining his features.

"Your guests won't be here for another hour right?"

His face was inches from hers. She could smell the cigarette smoke that clung to his clothes, and the beer he clearly had while watching the game.

"Uh-huh….," she trailed off, not sure what he was getting at.

Scott's fingers grazed bare skin above Haylee's waistband. "What should we do in the meantime?" he asked as he brushed his lips against her neck.

She might be naïve at times, but she understood his proposition. With her hands grasping his waist, she pushed Scott back a step. "I think we should just put our feet up until they get here." He cocked his head at her. "Kathy is always early," she added.

She could tell he was disappointed and it almost made her want to give in, but she didn't think she had enough time.

Defeated, he leaned up against the wall and did his best to extinguish the fire that had already built up inside. He folded his arms across his chest.

"Smells good. What are you making?" he asked.

"Lasagna. My world famous recipe."

He grimaced. "World famous? I've never heard about it."

Haylee plucked a beer from the refrigerator. "Well, you're about to," she proclaimed, handing him the can.

"We'll see." Scott happily took the beverage. "Thanks. You read my mind."

"Have you had a lot already?"

Scott's eyes rolled into the back of his head. "One or

two," he asserted. "I'll be fine." The can opened with a pop. "Aren't you going to have one?"

Haylee shook her head. "I'll wait and have a little of the wine Kathy is bringing."

She didn't have to wait long. Kathy predictably arrived early by thirty minutes, escorted by Jake. Wendy wasn't far behind, and Tom impressed her by showing up on time as well.

After the introductions had been made, Haylee had Scott help her light the fireplace she hadn't yet used. She kept her thermostat at a cool sixty seven degrees for the winter so her gas bill wouldn't soar. Haylee suspected the fire would not only be appreciated for the ambiance, but for the extra warmth as well.

Haylee poured and passed out wine while her guests chatted. She could tell from his body language that Scott was aggravated. Kathy and Wendy stood on either side of side of him asking questions, while Tom and Jake looked involved in hearty conversation. She warned him about the inquiries, her friends were anxious to get to know him aside from what she had told them.

The interrogation ceased a bit when they sat down to eat. Wendy and Tom were having their own discussion, while Kathy sat across from Scott and kept the dialogue rolling. Kathy's no-nonsense demeanor merely had her doing what came natural. She had been urged many times to become an attorney. She had a way of getting the information she wanted, whether or not it was offered freely. Scott had some smart-ass retorts to her, but Kathy wasn't fazed by it.

By the time they had dug into the lasagna, Jake dominated the table with his stories and jokes. Haylee mused how Kathy had failed to mention how humorous her date actually was. No one interrupted him while he spoke, but instead listened intently for the punch line or hilarious turn of events he would describe. She laughed so hard her stomach ached, and she noticed Kathy had to dab at the corner of her eyes a few times.

They took an intermission before dessert, and even then, Haylee had to coerce her friends into obliging her. No way was she going to be stuck with all the leftovers.

With their stomachs full, and the volume of their banter increasing, Haylee excused herself to the kitchen. Wendy was on her heels.

She gave her friend a hug. "Thanks for having me, everything was great. I'm afraid I need to be going."

Haylee nodded. "Okay. Glad you could come."

Wendy wanted to thank Scott for introducing her to Tom before she left, and caught him alone while Haylee was tidying up. Sitting down beside him on the couch, she watched him for a moment while he seemingly sized her up.

"Tom and I are going on a date next week. Thanks for setting us up."

A snicker escaped free from him. "Anytime." He was floored by the idea; she didn't look like the kind of girl to be interested in Tom. Too high maintenance. She wouldn't last long with him after she got to know him. He would bet on that.

Reading the confusion on her face, he immediately changed the subject. She would find it out on her own. "That's quite a getup you have there."

He was commenting on her attire. She had been told not to bother, it was her nature to dress a certain way. She saw it as an outward expression of her personality. She wore snug black cotton pants with a long silver tank top that was covered by a purple fitted sweater. Her beaded necklace was looped twice around her neck, but still hung down past her chest. And though she wasn't currently wearing them, her silver stilettos gave her an extra three inches of height. Her hair was pinned back neatly into a loose ponytail so that her red lipstick wouldn't be overpowering.

She turned away slightly as though it would compel him to look elsewhere. "I made it myself. Designed it, stitched it, everything. It was a project for one of my last classes. Guess I like to show off my work."

"Well it shows you off well too. Nice work." It slipped out unintentionally, but in truth, she looked picture perfect. He wondered if she was the kind of girl that would never go anywhere unless she was all made up. However irrational he found that to be, somehow those types of women attracted him, probably because of how striking they appeared after all their labor was complete.

She felt uneasy with his compliment. Glancing over her shoulder, no one was within earshot to hear their conversation. She chose to believe this was merely a friendly exchange, and took the flattery in stride.

"I appreciate it. It's commendable you were a sport about us grilling you. We were curious about the person that hooked Haylee. "

"I survived. I suppose it wasn't that bad. As long as it was a one-time thing."

Wendy held her hands up in defense. "Don't look at me. I'm through."

He nodded in relief. A few more similar sessions with them could have the potential to drive him crazy.

Haylee had mentioned Wendy's ambitions to him before. "You know, my friend from New York is into fashion design, and I know she has a lot of experience. I should introduce you two the next time she is in town, her family lives here. She'll probably be home for the holidays."

She was intrigued by the idea. "That would be great. It

never hurts to get some pointers from people who have been there. Good idea."

"I'll get a hold of you when I talk to her. We'll have lunch."

Less than a week lapsed before Scott got a hold of Wendy to inform her that his friend Sarah was in town. They were scheduled to meet shortly after her last class ended.

She had been busy all day studying for the exam she just had, and was relieved it was over. The test was in computer applications, a class that she was required to take in her curriculum. Computers were definitely not her forte, and therefore extra time to study the material was essential to her passing. She hoped she would never have to create a spreadsheet or PowerPoint presentation again.

She took her time walking the path through campus. She always took that route to meet Kathy, and normally arrived first. Once a week, they met for coffee since her last class on Thursday ended at five o'clock and the campus was on Kathy's way home from work. It was convenient for both of them and it gave them a chance to converse.

While she strolled along, Wendy examined the clothes people were wearing. She tried to deduce things about them based on their appearance. She was a firm believer that one's attire said a lot about a person. It was also amusing to her to observe the expressions on faces that went by. So many looked so serious, distressed even. Often she was baffled by how grumpy everyone seemed. Sure she had her moments, but she did her best to plaster a smile on her face at all times. Pouting never got her anywhere.

One passerby in particular caught her attention, crossing in front of her with a rapid pace. She adorned a tailored black suit and had a black leather briefcase slung over her shoulder. She was shouting into her cell phone. Her face demonstrated that she was dealing with a fairly large problem and was completely annoyed with whoever was on the other end of the phone line.

Wendy smirked to herself as she thought how the girl could use a little lipstick and needed to let her hair down out of the ponytail at the base of her head. Maybe letting out that tight pull would lighten her mood.

Glancing back as she moved forward, Wendy wondered how anyone lived with as much stress as that woman just exuded. Call her traditional, but Wendy chose to work for recreational amusement with the added benefit of a paycheck, and she would leave her future husband to deal with the stress associated with bringing in the big money. She would opt for fun and relaxation instead.

Opening the glass door to her destination, Kathy easily came into view when she waved her arms wildly in the air to get her friend's attention. Wendy plopped down in the seat across from her as Kathy pushed a large cup of steaming coffee forward.

Knowing her typical order, Kathy took it upon herself to get both of their drinks.

"You have to get your own cream and sugar. I would have surely put in the wrong ratio."

Wendy shook her head. "Wouldn't have been hard. Just put enough milk in that the color is white with a brown tint, and then add sugar until you think a child would be willing to drink it. It is the only way I can tolerate coffee."

As she poured generously into her cup, Kathy frowned. Wendy hadn't been exaggerating.

"Next time I'll just get you a soda. Probably less sugar in that."

"Nah. I only drink diet soda. Have to keep these pounds in check somehow," she claimed as she patted her hips. She made the switch some time ago when her weight slowly began to increase as she got older. It was still a constant battle to keep the numbers on the scale where they already were, let alone go back down to where they used to be.

"How did you beat me here?" Wendy asked.

"I left a few minutes early today. I had about all I could take for the day."

Wendy slurped her drink unintentionally that was no longer hot. "Yeah? One of those days?"

Kathy snorted. "Like every day. It's a good thing I know how to flip the switch the instant I walk out of my employer's door. Otherwise, our beverages might have needed to be of the adult variety."

"Well, that will be my next stop. I'm meeting Scott and his friend in a bit." She told Kathy of the purpose of the gathering. Which led her to her next question.

"So what do you think of Scott anyway?"

Tapping a finger to her mouth as though contemplating, she finally came up with a response. "I'm not sure."

Intrigued, as Kathy most always had a quick opinion, Wendy probed further. "Why not?"

"Well, seeing as Haylee is happy and thinks highly of him, I am compelled to try my hardest to like him. But there is something about him that screams jerk if you ask me."

Somewhat relieved that maybe she hadn't been hallucinating, Wendy nodded in agreement. "I was thinking the same. It doesn't appear as though he is a one-woman type of guy, and I felt as though he was flirting with me a little at Haylee's party. Please don't take that as arrogance."

Kathy narrowed her eyes. "Let me say first that I don't take that as arrogance." She knew her well enough to believe that Wendy wouldn't make that up or falsely interpret the situation. The girly girl had plenty of experience of being hit on to realize when it was happening. "But now it makes me wonder. The description seems fitting. I just don't want to see Haylee get hurt. She has always been such a recluse to the dating world that it would almost be tragic to watch her first real attempt go down in flames. I'm not sure she could handle it."

Wendy hoped they were wrong. "When you are on the outside looking in, it is so much easier to see problems and other things that you can't manage to see when you are immersed in it. That's one of the reasons why I have my doubts, but maybe we're mistaken. We only just met him."

Snap judgments weren't exactly fair, but in Kathy's experience, somehow frighteningly accurate. "Guess we'll have to see."

Chapter 10

$\mathcal{H}$aylee couldn't help but to feel uneasy that Scott was leaving to meet with two ladies, one her friend, without her. She tried hard to swallow the twinge of jealously that was in her throat.

Sprawling out on his queen size bed, silently pouting to herself, she folded her arms beneath her chin, facing the work clothes Scott had just thrown atop the blankets. She had come by unexpectedly after a particularly exhausting day at the office, intending to spend the rest of the day relaxing with him on the couch in front of the television. But to her dismay, he had already made plans.

"How about you just go tomorrow instead?" she asked hopefully.

"Can't. We are going to the casino with Kathy and Jake tomorrow, remember?"

"Oh yeah. Next week then?" It was feeble she knew, but she didn't want to be alone. She needed someone to vent to, and he was the likely candidate.

"Aren't you the one that always says how you can't stand

when someone makes plans with you then breaks them at the last minute?" It was an attempt to get through to her rational side and past her complaining.

Lowering her eyes, he had unveiled her contradiction. "Yes."

"Well then. Aren't you asking me to be that person to someone else?"

She had the look of a scorned child that had just been punished. "I guess so."

"It's settled then. I'll call you when I get home and we can talk then." It was written all over her face that she was upset. "Sarah isn't in town often and I told Wendy I would introduce them. I am going along because I haven't seen Sarah in quite some time. It's not like I am going on a date."

"I know. But it would have been nice if you had asked me to go." She had the notion of inviting herself along, but dismissed the idea. He didn't give any indication that was an option.

She just wasn't going to quit, was she? To appease her, and to change the subject, he suggested, "If you don't mind that it will be pretty late, I'll come over afterward."

She perked up slightly and dropped the direction in which she was going. "That would be great in fact. I don't mind."

Haylee reached into her pocket. "Here take this. I had it made for you." She placed the silver house key into his hand, and rising up off the bed, came around behind him. With her arms wrapped around his waist, up on her tiptoes, she gazed at him through the mirror in front of which they stood. "Love you."

He lifted his eyes from his palm, with a grin. "Love you too."

Sarah was diligently typing into her laptop computer when Scott approached her. Wrapped up in what she was doing, she didn't even notice him.

"Ahem. Mind if I take a seat?"

She jumped up to give him a hug. "Of course not! Glad to see you."

"Likewise. Busy there?"

"I was returning some e-mails. It is hard to be out of town. Everyone seems to need something from you precisely when you are not around."

"Nah, I am sure they can wait. Is it really life or death if your seamstress is out of purple ribbon?"

Sneering, she dished it right back. It was essentially the foundation of their friendship. "No. But I guess in your case it would be. Do all your clients have enough band-aids?"

He narrowed his eyes. "My company's provisions are a bit more high-tech than band-aids. But you already know that."

Scott slid his chair close to Sarah's. Their relationship was atypical. Their short stint at a romantic love affair failed, yet depending on their moods, they hadn't fully abandoned the physical aspect of it. They dated other people, and called themselves friends, but were closer than that. Despite the similarities they shared, they couldn't commit to each other.

"So, you do remember the plan?"

Sighing, Sarah proclaimed, "You are relentless. Yes, I am to chitchat with her for awhile and bore you to death with the details of fashion design. Then suddenly I remember I am to be at my parents' house for dinner and dash out of here."

Throwing an arm around her, he gave her a quick squeeze. "You are the best. Kind of like my female wingman."

She stuck her finger in her mouth and made a gagging noise. "Mm-hmm. I thought you were all about that other girl, what was her name? I can't keep up. Oh yeah, Haylee."

"I am. But you know I like to play the field and see what's out there. Just in case."

She knew. She had watched for several years now. "What you need is a woman to set you straight, make a man out of you yet," she declared as she maternally pinched his cheek.

"And I suppose that would be you?"

It was a thought that had crossed Sarah's mind many times. The imprudent belief that she could be the one girl to change him. A challenge it would be no doubt, but one she could surely conquer. One day, she might dare.

"Who else? Who else has enough resolve to manage you?"

"You talk a mean talk, but I don't think you have it in you."

Before she could argue her point, Scott was rising to greet who must be Wendy. No wonder Scott was interested. Sarah had to admit, Wendy looked picture perfect.

Sarah played along and did what he had asked of her. Before leaving, Sarah passed out her phone number so Wendy could keep in touch. They had quite a few things in common, and it was always nice for Sarah to make a new friend since she didn't have many that were women. She felt a little sorry that Wendy was going to be a subject of Scott's target, and hoped that Wendy upheld Sarah's estimation that she had a decent head on her shoulders.

Watching her go, Wendy turned to face Scott. "Guess I'll get going too. I'm sure you have other things to do."

Scott gulped down the last of his beer before lighting a cigarette. "I don't really. I had assumed we would be here much longer, seeing as you two had plenty to talk about.

It's too bad Sarah had to run, I don't get to see her often."
Lifting his glass to signal their waitress over, Scott suggested,
"Why don't you stay and have another drink with me?"

She had only planned on the one she already finished,
but she thought it rude to get up and leave after he had been
nice enough to set up this little meeting. "Alright, only one
more for me. I have to get up early."

"Sure." He blew off her assertion and planned his
strategy to change her mind as he checked the time.

"I'll be right back. I need to use the ladies' room."

As she walked off to the restroom, Scott placed their
drink order, and was sure to include a request for two shots
of tequila in addition to the beer he ordered for himself and
the fruity mixed drink for Wendy. He would venture to
guess that the tequila would have her more than a little tipsy.
Then maybe she would let her guard down some.

When she returned, the shock mixed with disgust on
her face had him snickering. "Problem?"

"You order all that for yourself or do you expect me to
help you? Either way, not good."

"Oh come on. That's the thanks I get for buying you
a drink? I figured you could knock one back with me in
appreciation." With that, he only got a slight moan in
response. "I see how it is. I'll remember that. Wendy gets
prudish when it comes to showing her gratitude…"

She cut him off midsentence. Politely she said, "Thank
you. I didn't mean it that way. It's just the last time I drank
tequila….oh never mind." Peer pressure was a bitch. She
prayed she wouldn't regret it later. "What shall we drink
to?"

Although he was curious to know about that last time
she drank tequila and the outcome of the situation, he merely
said, with a barely detectable amount of sarcasm that Wendy

did not pick up, "To the exciting world of fashion." With that he picked up his shot glass, waiting for her response.

She perked up as this toast was not expected, and it was odd to come from his mouth. As she hesitatingly wrapped her hand around the small glass containing the vile liquor, she wrinkled her nose. "Interesting choice. What made you say that?"

He put on his most charming grin that had him looking strangely sexy. "Would we be here otherwise?" Then he added, "Now we have the opportunity to have a little fun after business. So cheers."

He had time to finish his, and still be able to watch her plug her nose as she poured the liquid down her throat with an expression that couldn't be described as anything less than excruciating. Instead of slamming the glass down in a triumphant gesture, he noticed the goose bumps that had formed on her arms as she shuddered and put the lime forcefully in her mouth. The sour fruit had her lips puckering.

Slowly recovering Wendy demanded, "Okay. Sorry, but no more of those. I won't make it."

Scott let a howl of laughter loose. "I'll let you slide this time. After that reaction, I couldn't dream of making you do it again."

His laugh was contagious and Wendy joined in to poke fun at herself even though she was embarrassed. "I don't suppose that was the most flattering illustration of myself, but that's what you get for egging me on!" She felt more at ease now, but was still mostly uncomfortable. For reasons she couldn't pinpoint, he made her uneasy.

It hadn't been that long, but Haylee was already becoming impatient. There was only so much she felt like doing at the moment to keep herself occupied. She had taken the long, hot bath she promised herself, read several chapters in the novel she was reading, and had eaten a tasty dinner of Chinese food that she had delivered. Flipping through the channels, there was nothing worthwhile on the television to peak her interest.

She even caught herself drumming her fingers atop the book on her lap in a true act of boredom. Now instead, she began picking at her fingernails where the polish was starting to chip.

The frustration of the day had finally ceased for the most part. At least she had accomplished that much. Normally, she could get over problems quickly and brush them off with little effort on her own, but she hadn't completely shaken off the need to be comforted by Scott. Most likely, her frustration had only been buried to be replaced by a dull annoyance in Scott. She dealt with the fact he wasn't available when she wanted him to be, needed him to be, but she strongly felt like the least he could have done was make his outing brief and rush home to her.

Telling herself she wouldn't blow up at him when he finally arrived, she picked up her phone to check for missed calls. Maybe she had not heard the phone ring. No luck.

It was becoming a habit, she knew. He would be out, and tell her he would call or come over at a certain time but undershoot the estimate by hours. When she would try to contact him there would be no answer. Then the same stories, "I lost track of time, I left my cell phone in the car," etc.

She had at one point asked him if she wasn't important at all. He had completely reassured her that she was, but now again, she wasn't so sure. How many times did she have to convey to him how lousy it made her feel in order for him to change the behavior?

Two buttons pushed, and the call was being made. She

had put his number on speed dial a long while back. On occasion, when she had waited for so long, she had dialed over and over again to no avail. Only once tonight. Then she was headed for bed.

She berated herself silently. No wonder she had avoided getting involved with anyone for so long. Relationships were so much work. It could make a person crazy she thought.

Even though she began to see it was useless, she listened while the ringing tone repeated itself again and again. Finally, his voicemail picked up and she hung up without leaving a message.

She had nothing to say at the moment.

After he had hit the ignore button to silence the call, he held down the power button to shut the phone off. It was likely that she would try again, so he would avoid it altogether and say his battery had died.

"Was that Haylee? She must be wondering where you are."

Stuffing the phone back into his pocket, he responded, "No, it was my Mom. I'll call her back later. I told Haylee I would be late so she's not expecting me."

Wendy shifted in her chair and leaned back to stretch out her legs. She was feeling good she had to admit, with the haze of a tequila-flavored cloud around her head.

But she could see where this little interlude was going. She wasn't dumb after all. The last thing she wanted was the interest from one of her good friends' boyfriends. He had just given it away by saying Haylee wasn't expecting him. She certainly was, as the text message she had sent indicated, "try not to keep my man too long!" Wendy had checked her messages when she had walked away from the table.

He must believe she had no loyalty, no sense of integrity. On the other hand, it could just be that he is ignorant and overconfident in himself with an ego the size of a small city. She decided it was a mixture of both.

She would play along. She wanted to make sure she was right in her assessment. If it was true, she wanted him to be overtly obvious about it. Haylee didn't need this kind of schmuck in her life. Better to reveal it now rather than later. He made a mistake in choosing to go after a close friend.

"It's getting late. Why don't you walk me to my car?" Wendy asked with a sly look on her face.

Hmmph. He had been right. He would test the waters. "I could take you home instead since you have been drinking."

Not wanting the test to go that far, she declined. "Maybe some other time." Geez, hadn't he had more to drink than her anyway? The free pretzels she had been snacking on were doing their job to soak up what she had consumed. Thinking of an excuse, she alleged, "I would pass out on you anyway, and what fun would that be? Better to wait."

He could handle that, the door had at least been opened.

As they walked out to where her car was parked, he told her, "We should get together again soon."

Her only thought was, yeah right. "Mmm-hmm." She wanted to keep the charade going.

She paused before getting in the driver's seat and faced him. He grasped her hand and pulled her forward while leaning his head down to her. It happened fast and she didn't have time to stop him before his lips were planted on hers, and his hands were wandering over her body.

Wriggling loose of him, she laid her forearms on his chest and gave a shove out of revulsion. He was knocked off balance and went back a few steps and stared at her in confusion.

Sneering at him, she barked, "So this is how you really

are? You are an ass. Especially since you believed I would go along with it. Haylee genuinely cares about you. But obviously you don't give a fuck."

This was unexpected. He hadn't seen it coming, the turn in her behavior. Apparently she had a small talent for acting in her because she had him fooled into thinking she was interested. Now, to play his cards right, he would need to begin damage control.

"I'm sorry. You are completely right. I don't know what I was thinking."

The expression on her face told him she wasn't buying it. "I made a mistake. Let's just leave it at that and forget it."

"Sorry isn't going to cut it. I don't believe you are being sincere. Wait until Haylee hears, she is going to kick you to the curb."

She turned to get into the car, but Scott grabbed her wrist.

His temper was beginning to flare, and he set his jaw and breathed deep to attempt to keep it in check. "Look, I think its best if this stays between us. Besides, how would it look for you when I tell her how you made passes at me all night, but then had a sudden attack of conscience?"

"Doesn't matter because that's not the truth."

"Shall we see what truth she buys? I'll bet she'll take my word over yours."

"Whatever. Good luck with that." The car door slammed shut behind her and she wasted no time driving off. She and Haylee had been friends for years and she'd be damned if Haylee took Scott's word over hers. Looking at the clock, Wendy decided to talk to Haylee now since it was still early, although she had no idea how to convey the news. Um, hi, your boyfriend is a cheat? She would figure it out. Scott was probably on his way over to her house, and Wendy wanted to tell her before Scott had the chance to fill her head with lies.

As she slammed her phone down, tears of rage and hurt threatened to pour down from her eyes.

How dare Wendy come up with a lie like that?

The door flew open and Scott came through. He smiled, giving no indication something was wrong. She knew Wendy had to have been imagining things, and that she overreacted to something Scott did or said.

He kicked off his black dress shoes and removed his black leather coat while Haylee struggled to remain collected. She had almost convinced herself that it wasn't true, that Scott did not have eyes for anyone but her. But the shred of doubt would not shake itself off without his assertion.

Inside, her stomach had dropped when the words came out of her friend's mouth. Instinctively, on some level, she recognized the possibility, but her head had talked her into accepting what she wanted to believe was true. She just needed the final reassurance.

A jumble of emotions, she blurted, "I am going to get right to it. What happened tonight? Do you need to tell me anything? Why is Wendy calling me saying all these awful things? I thought you and Wendy were meeting up with one of your friends."

Scott did his best to display shock. Wendy hadn't wasted any time ratting on him. He had mistakenly assumed she would have trouble bringing that information forward out of some sort of guilt.

"Whoa." He held up his hands, feeling bombarded. "Okay. One question at a time. Yes, we met with Sarah, who had to leave abruptly because she had forgotten she was to meet her parents for dinner."

He paused, but Haylee said nothing. "Wendy and I had

a drink since it was still early. I didn't want to be rude and run off as soon as Sarah left. We left shortly thereafter."

Considering, Haylee narrowed her gaze and fixed it upon him. "That's it?"

"With the exception of the finer details, yes. Unless you want to hear the specifics about the content of our conversation."

She paused a moment, letting what he said sink in. Giving one last try, she warned, "Don't lie."

He covered his tracks with ease. "What else do you expect?"

She remembered another reason she was mad. "I tried to call you. You didn't answer. Why would that be if you weren't 'busy' with someone else?"

"Haylee, my phone battery died leaving it without power. It shut itself off because I forgot to charge it yesterday. My mistake."

She was guilty of doing the same on occasion, so it made sense. She had been so angry, but with a few words, he had extinguished her temper.

He embraced her, and her initial reaction was to retreat. The hurt was nonetheless lingering, although she felt better now that he had given his account. When she instead chose to lean into his shoulder, the scent of smoke in his clothes had her nose wrinkling.

He told her, "I love you."

Her response was fast, "I love you too, but…"

"But what? What did Wendy say?"

Feeling ashamed to voice her claim, Haylee considered trying to just drop the subject. But he pressed on.

Bowing her head down to avoid his eyes, she told him Wendy's allegations.

Sneering at her words, he declared, "That's ridiculous.

She doesn't know what she is talking about. Why would I do something like that when I have you?"

She had wondered that herself, only to come up with the idea that maybe she had done something wrong.

"I don't know. I figured you were upset with me for some reason."

"I wasn't upset. Although it would be nice if you could be more understanding when I tell you I have plans, and that I can't always be available to you at the drop of a hat."

She sulked to herself. "Sorry. I'll do my best."

"Good. Now why don't we go lie down? You can tell me all about your day."

Chapter 11

$\mathcal{T}$he next day, Haylee skipped going to the office. She had nothing major planned, so she sent some marketing flyers in the mail and sent a few follow-up e-mails from home.

She had felt comforted falling asleep in Scott's arms the night before after venting to him about her stressful day. Despite their squabble, Haylee had recovered quickly. He had her trust and she had all but forgotten why she had even doubted him in the first place. She would have a talk with Wendy and hopefully get the misunderstanding straightened out.

Perhaps because she wanted to draw Scott closer to her, or maybe because she felt it was the next logical step, whatever the reason, she had asked him to move in with her that morning. His apartment lease was coming to an end and she wouldn't mind having the extra income to help her pay the mortgage. The financial details were trivial she had said, and they could be figured out later. He had gladly accepted.

Wasting no time, she had urged him to begin bringing

his things over, little by little. He had three weeks left before he had to officially move out of his apartment, and luckily had not yet renewed his lease.

Haylee was a mixture of excitement and anxiety. She had lived on her own for quite some time, and had little knowledge of what it would be like living with a man. However, they spent most nights together so she couldn't see how it could be *that* different. She had grown so accustomed to his company that she couldn't help but to be happy they would be under the same roof.

She stared out the window from behind her computer, contemplating how the move would affect their relationship. Needing some air, she cracked open the pane, letting a cool breeze through that countered the heat her computer was pushing out. The melodic tune of a robin's song was now audible, though it was offset by nearby traffic.

She rose to fill her coffee mug one last time, almost tripping over a pair of Scott's shoes that were strewn across the floor. She scowled out loud, noting one change the move would bring.

The plan for later was to meet Kathy and Jake at Kathy's house so they could drive together to a nearby casino boat. She wasn't much of a gambler, but she thought it might be fun to watch everyone else blow their money. She decided to take a modest fifty dollars with her, just so she wouldn't be left out.

By the time Scott had finished moving some boxes over to Haylee's, which he set down in the spare bedroom without unpacking, he barely had enough time to take a quick shower before they had to leave. Since she had had plenty of time, Haylee was patiently waiting, all set to go as soon as he was ready.

He finished quickly, but realized he had forgotten to stop and withdraw cash from his bank account.

"That's fine we'll run to an ATM," Haylee told him.

"I lost my card, remember? I'd have to go through the teller. I don't think my bank is open at six o'clock on Friday night."

Already late, Haylee was struggling not to lose her patience. "I don't think any are. I'll loan you the cash. We'll stop on the way."

Cash obtained, driving as fast as she dared, Haylee arrived at Kathy's twenty minutes late. Always the one to be blamed, Haylee told Scott, "This one's on you. You were the one running behind, and I am going to have this small victory of no fault."

As Kathy and Jake came outside to pile in Haylee's car, Kathy gave her a look.

Knowing the implication, Haylee pointed the finger at Scott.

"Not my fault," she claimed.

Scott sighed, exasperated. "It was mine," he asserted.

When they got to their destination, the group optimistically vowed they would leave with more cash than they came with. It was irrational, but they still made bets on who would win the most.

The women went their own way, leaving the guys to a cloud of smoke around the blackjack table. Scott insisted it was the only way to ensure any kind of winnings in the entire casino, and thought Haylee foolish for wanting to hit the slot machines.

Haylee sized up a line of machines, randomly choosing one she hoped was lucky. The bright lights atop the apparatus promised large sums of money for a jackpot win. The seats in her aisle were pretty empty so there was little competition if she wanted to move around.

Shaking her head, Kathy plopped down in the seat beside her and slid a twenty dollar bill into the cash feed.

She figured at least it would take awhile to get through a twenty since each pull was only a quarter.

"You are not going to blow all your money sitting at these slots are you?" Kathy asked her.

Letting out a yelp of laughter, she alleged, "I thought we were all winning, right?"

"True. But I don't think this is the way to go. Aren't the odds horrible with these?"

Haylee shrugged. "I don't really know how to play anything else, and besides, I didn't bring a whole lot of money to spend."

"We'll have to check on the guys here shortly, and see how they are doing. If Jake is up, I am going to grab some of his chips and head over to the roulette table. I'm sure he won't mind," she said matter-of-factly.

"Talk about blowing money. Maybe he'd want to hang on to his winnings."

Kathy shook her head. "He said he wouldn't care. I already joked about it before we left when he was bragging about his good luck in gambling. Said that way, I won't dip into my grocery budget. A girl has got to eat you know." Contemplating, Haylee decided she might have to ask the same if Scott was ahead. After all, he was playing with money she had lent him. And who could miss dollars they didn't have in the first place?

"That's a good idea. Sounds like Jake is pretty agreeable."

"He is. A little frivolous with his finances right now, but I think that is the bachelor in him. But, we have been talking about how that might change soon."

Haylee raised her eyebrows. "Oh? What do you mean?" Kathy had mentioned before that the two of them wanted to live together since they practically did already. Their address was not the same, but they didn't spend a night apart.

"I think we will get married. Eventually. No rush."

A little surprised, Haylee asked, "You think so? I guess I didn't realize it was so serious."

Kathy had become aware that they had been so involved in their own lives that the two of them hadn't had much time to talk. "It is. I think we will be engaged soon."

"Wow. That's great. Happened so fast."

It was true, and it made Kathy a little nervous, only because she usually wasn't so speedy in the process. She used to believe that these things took time, but Jake had proved her wrong.

"I'm aware of that, but when you find that person, you just know."

Haylee wasn't so sure, but then again, she didn't have a whole lot of experience either. A relationship seemed too complicated to be able to figure everything out in a short amount of time.

"Well, I am happy for you! You'll have to fill me in when it happens so we can officially celebrate."

Kathy lit up with excitement. "You know I will! You can help me start planning."

As Haylee pulled the lever of her slot machine for the hundredth time, she smiled at her friend. She was so happy. "I have some good news of my own. Scott is moving in."

It was Kathy's turn to be surprised that progress was possible. "Now that's something. You go from commitment phoebe to making such a large step. He really got you to come around huh?"

"He did. I have felt comfortable enough to let my guard down to explore a serious relationship. I love him. And it makes sense. We are together so often. No need to pay a mortgage and rent."

Kathy listened to her friend's logic. "True. But the main

reason is because you think it would be a good step for you, right?"

Haylee was quick to reassure. "Of course. Don't get the wrong idea. I uh, I know it will work out and bring us closer."

Encouraging her, Kathy declared, "Well you want to test drive the car before you buy."

Haylee liked the comparison. "Sure do. Want to make sure it doesn't crap out the instant I get it home," she joked.

Kathy could sense an anxiety in Haylee, but chalked it up to her friend fretting over the changes. It was a big step that could make anyone a little nervous.

When the money they put into the slots ran out, they decided to check in on their dates. The casino had begun to fill up by then, and it took a little work to weave through the people who were standing in the aisles trying to figure out where to gamble next. Haylee commented that she would prefer if smoking was not allowed inside, knowing they were going to smell like ashtrays by the time they left.

Halfway to the blackjack table, a loud cheer came from their right. An older woman was jumping up and down while trying to hug the man she was with at the same time. From the look of her elated face, she must have won a decent amount. The pit boss was clapping for her, as were the other patrons surrounding them. Kathy joked that the two of them could take her, perhaps they should jump her and take the chips and run.

They approached the area where Scott and Jake were sitting. It appeared as though they hadn't moved an inch since the girls had left them. Both had drinks in hand, Scott with a vodka and tonic, Jake with a pilsner. They were talking animatedly, giving a good indication that they were getting along well. Haylee and Kathy crept up behind them, looking over their shoulders to see how they were doing with the game.

"Well boys, are we up?" Kathy asked.

Jake turned to pull her down to his level to kiss her. Happily, he admitted, "We are. I am up one hundred, but Mr. Scott here is up twice that."

Kathy and Haylee exchanged a glance with their eyebrows raised. Kathy smacked Scott on the shoulder. "Wow, impressive. We will be calling you moneybags by the time we leave here. And, we'll be trying to bum dinner off you too."

Scott wasn't finished yet and was prepared to keep on going. "Only problem is, we haven't been able to leave the table. I've got to piss like a racehorse."

Haylee furrowed her brow, and gave Scott a light slap on the arm. "Ew, nice language there." Scott rolled his eyes at Jake, while Haylee withheld the comment she wanted to make about Scott having drinks so often. "Guess that's the price you pay. Should have worn a diaper." She snickered. "I hear some people actually do that."

Jake stood up, gathering his earnings. "Not me. I'll take that as my cue to have a break, and make another go at it in awhile."

Reluctantly, Scott got out of his chair too and joined the group. "It will be a quick break for me. I want to get back while I am on a roll."

Haylee linked arms with Scott. "On a lucky streak I see. Why don't we go gamble some of those chips together? You can tell me what to call at roulette."

He dismissed the idea. "No way. We'll be sure to lose it all in twenty minutes. I am coming back to blackjack. Best odds."

Even though he didn't want to make Scott look bad, Jake wanted to make the girls happy. Knowing Kathy had that thought in mind too, he turned to her. "I'll go with you for a little while, but I would eventually like to rejoin Scott."

He told Scott, "Why don't we go over there with them for a bit, satisfy their apparent need to burn through cash, and we'll head back over together shortly?"

His immediate thought was to call Jake a sucker. But he resisted. "Fine. But I am not placing any bets. No point. Might as well make stabs in the dark, you'd have better luck."

Haylee told him, "I can place them then." She pressed her fingers to her temple. "I'll use my keen sense of intuition."

"How about not," Scott came back. "This is free money here, and I can think of several things that I would like to buy and splurge on while I have the chance."

Haylee thought it selfish. After all, they were there just to have some fun. Scott was clearly taking it more seriously. She was a bit mad, until she remembered it was his money and that she had only lent some to him for the moment. "Alright," she said. "We'll watch Kathy and Jake and give them some pointers."

"Works for me," he said.

They watched on as Kathy thoughtfully chose her numbers to bet, concentrating as to what her gut told her. Thirty minutes later, she was still even to what she started with. She would win one, and then inevitably lose one or two more. It was entertaining to her at least, especially since she hadn't immediately lost out. The group egged her on and gave their suggestions from time to time. Scott stood next to Haylee and kept shifting his weight and huffing under his breath.

Finally, Haylee turned to him aggravated, but understanding. "Why don't you head back to poker and continue your winning streak."

"It was blackjack. But yes, I think I'll get back to it, if that's okay with you." He said it snotty to her.

"Right. Sorry to keep you. I didn't realize you would be so bored."

He didn't respond, but hastily kissed her forehead and ran off.

Jake didn't need a degree in women's studies to recognize the look Haylee was exuding. It asked him, however politely, to please leave. He took his cue. "I am going to follow Scott. See you in a bit. Good luck by the way."

She squeezed the hand of his that she had been holding and then let go. "Same to you. You just go ahead and leave this hundred bucks with me."

"I suppose. I better get something good out of it," he teased. He was smirking at her.

"Hmm. We'll see." There was no question in her mind that he would.

When Jake was out of earshot, and Kathy had placed her bets, awaiting the next number called, she glanced over to Haylee. She was upset, but hiding it fairly well.

"What's his problem?" Kathy asked her.

Her instinct was to defend him. "I think he is a little grouchy from stress. I know he had a tough week at work."

Kathy was beginning to think that it was just his personality to be grouchy, but she kept that to herself.

"Well that sucks. We'll have to teach him to leave work at the door when he goes home."

Trying to not let a few minor setbacks spoil her night, she brushed off Scott's behavior. "Yeah. Yeah we will."

Kathy wanted to change the subject to alleviate Haylee's tension, but incidentally chose the wrong topic. "How's your Mom?" Kathy had always been fond of and close to Haylee's mother, and hadn't seen her in awhile.

Frowning, Haylee thought about lying in order to avoid

her feelings, but didn't. "Not so good at the moment. She had a big blowout with my Dad about some money that he apparently owes her. He was supposed to split my college bills with her. He began to pay her back little by little, but has fallen behind again. Mom wouldn't fuss so much over it, but she needs to pay off the medical bills."

Diane was in a car accident the prior year that required a stay in the hospital. She had unintentionally had a lapse in her health insurance, thinking she had paid the extension to cover her while she had waited for her new employer's coverage to kick in. That hadn't been the case, and therefore, she wasn't given any monetary assistance. She had to undergo surgery, had a broken wrist, and needed a few stitches on her arm. It had cost her a small fortune. She was dipping into her savings to make the minimum payments to the hospital.

Still a sore spot for her, Haylee did her best to ignore her father's existence. He had never been there for her and had left her and her Mom years before. She found it appalling that Ken could leave a part of his life behind, never to give a second thought to it, and throw it all away. The two women who should have been the most important in his life were merely past acquaintances. Resentment held strong in her and slowly poisoned her heart over the years. She was doing her best these days to flush it clean, but supposed that's why she found it so easy to keep men at a distance.

"I offered to help Mom out, but she won't have it," Haylee added.

The number twenty five was called and ten of Kathy's chips were pulled away from the loss. She sat out a round to focus her attention on Haylee. The only anger her friend typically expressed was when she spoke of Ken.

"What a jerk. We should ransack his house and find any way we can to sabotage him. And, of course, your Mom wouldn't take the financial help. Isn't that where you get it from?"

"Yeah, I guess. And as much as he might deserve it, we'll do no sabotaging." Haylee couldn't muster the will to purposely hurt anyone. "Let's not talk about it. Speaking of him never fails to get me down."

Nodding, Kathy said, "Let's go for a big win here. What number should we play?"

Contemplating, Haylee finally chose. She had considered a lucky number, but then those never seemed to work. "Eight," she asserted. Since Ken was on her mind, she chose the age when he hit the hills.

"Alright. We'll put seventy five dollars on it. That's almost all I have left. Fifty fifty split. But don't hold your breath."

Sliding the stacks of five dollar tokens over, they looked like a mountain heaped atop the small box containing their selection. The pit boss waved his hand over the table to signal no more bets were to be placed. The girls crossed their fingers, knowing full well it was a ten-second thrill that would be lost in a few moments.

The ball was set loose and spun around the numbered wheel. Kathy turned her face away and closed her eyes. It wasn't a large amount of money relative to the casino. They saw bets placed that were astronomically higher. But for someone her age, seventy five dollars was a fair amount to throw away at a roulette table.

It bounced around on its bumpy ride, passing numbers, then finally settled in a slot. Haylee clapped excitedly when it stopped, giving it a few seconds to be sure it didn't move somehow on her. Kathy squinted open her eyes.

"Eight black." It was announced.

Kathy's jaw dropped. Now she wished she had had more chips to place on eight. It wasn't often you got this lucky, and she was fairly certain it would never happen to them again. She looked at her friend. "Nice call."

They high-fived each other and clasped hands gleefully. Haylee said about the 'unlucky' number, "I guess good can come from bad."

The payout received was a little over twenty five hundred dollars. Not a bad day's work. They both expressed how it would be nice to always make that much in such a short time.

The girls gathered their winnings and called it quits. They agreed that it wouldn't get better than what they had. A brief moment passed where Kathy suggested they try to get even more, but rationality won out and they went to seek out their blackjack players.

Kathy alleged she was going to spend most of the money on a day trip to the spa and urged Haylee to go with her. The rest she was going to buy a nice gift for Jake since if it hadn't been for his generosity, she would be sitting empty handed.

More conscientious, Haylee considered the proposition without committing to it. She imagined it would be nice to splurge and pamper herself. If she wanted to cut costs, she could only stay half as long as Kathy would, she mused. She only told Kathy, "We'll figure something out."

Scott and Jake were impressed by the win. Jake told them, "Now I am kicking myself in the ass for leaving and not giving everything to you. I am not doing as well as before."

Haylee said, "You gotta know when to fold 'em right? I had to pull Kathy away before she had any crazy ideas."

Kathy shrugged. "I only wanted to keep the fun going, that's all."

Since Jake was down and Scott was growing tiresome, they decided to call it a night. They stopped to eat at the casino's steakhouse before leaving since none of them had bothered with dinner thus far. The menu prices weren't cheap, but none of them minded with the extra cash in their pockets.

Haylee watched as Kathy and Jake visibly doted on one another during dinner. From all she could tell, Jake was a nice guy and clearly fond of Kathy. More than fond really, he appeared crazy about her, and she was guilty of the same. She hadn't seen Kathy act this way without hesitation, and Kathy would be the first to admit she had a problem staying engaged with one person for an extended amount of time. Whether she lost interest, or he couldn't deal with some of her intense personality traits, one way or another the flame extinguished fairly quickly. But theirs only appeared to grow.

From Kathy's point of view, she was observing almost the exact opposite. Scott looked as though he was lost out in space, brushing Haylee off as she tried to get closer to him. He seemed different now then when she had first met him at Haylee's party. He had been all over her then and had been attentive. Now he was picking at his steak, and staying out of the conversation to the best of his ability. She wondered what had brought on the change, or if it was temporary, perhaps over some issue tonight. Whatever it was, Kathy had decided that she did not care for this individual.

It might be a hasty conclusion, but it was Kathy's way. Some considered it a curse, and others a gift, but the fact of the matter was that she had a very good determination of character even when based on limited information. It was her experience that her first impressions were right. She didn't care for Scott's antics, or the veil of arrogance that he carried around him like a fashion accessory. She tried to give him the benefit of the doubt seeing as though Haylee thought highly of him, but to no avail. Kathy lacked the naiveté Haylee had when it came to people, and she believed Scott's moral fibers were thinner than most.

Kathy's resolve was only strengthened when the bill for dinner came. The waiter was kind enough to split the check into two for each of the couples, giving them to Scott and Jake. Jake threw down cash, but Scott passed his slip over to Haylee. Scott's assertion was that Haylee should pick up the tab since she had won more money. It was only fair, he had said. His demeanor and the ice in his voice told them all it was not up for debate. Reluctantly, Haylee did so, saying she saw his point.

After dropping Kathy and Jake off, Scott and Haylee headed home. She was perturbed by Scott's behavior during their outing, but chose not to say much of it until they were alone because she didn't want to make a scene.

She broached the subject gently, without making accusations. "Was there something wrong with you tonight?"

"Nope. Just fine. Why?"

"I don't know." Okay, forget not accusing she thought. "You were awful selfish tonight, only doing what Scott wanted to do. And you were very quiet. I felt as though you were withdrawn from the rest of the group. You pulled away when I would try to get close to you."

"You know I don't like being overly affectionate in public. It's tacky. We don't need to prove anything."

She didn't think it tacky. Some people went overboard with public displays, but all she was talking about here was as simple as an embrace or a peck on the lips, nothing major.

"And I wasn't trying to be selfish, only logical. I expressed my thoughts to you, that I was there to win, not lose, and I was taking the best route possible. It's not my idea of a good time to purposely throw money down the toilet, though that's what usually happens. We were a rare exception."

Haylee noted to herself that it was not a place to frequent with Scott for entertainment. "I guess we see things different in those regards. Do you understand where I am coming from though? Can you go with the flow a little more?"

Scott was in no mood to argue with her. He didn't see the problem with the guys going their own way, and it was hard enough to socialize with people who were still strangers to him. He had done his best with Kathy and Jake. He conversed so much with people at work through the week that all he wanted on weekends was the ability to be introverted. He supposed she was right about him pulling away from her, but he just hadn't felt like being close.

"Yeah, I'll do my best." At that, he leaned over to kiss her cheek, then down on her neck.

"Alright, enough of that. I'm still driving here."

"Fine. I'll wait until we get home to finish."

Chapter 12

$\mathcal{T}$he following morning, Haylee had appointments scheduled all day for home viewings. She had yet to meet the client because he had been a referral to her broker from a company in Arizona. Relocation referrals were alternated between agents, depending upon expertise in the client's desired area of town and upon sheer availability.

Pete Riley had come into town the day before for a job interview, but it had only been a formality to sign paperwork to accept the position. He had called earlier in the week to request that someone in the office show him around that Saturday, and Haylee had jumped on the opportunity. Not only was she one of the few agents still used to working every Saturday, but it had been mentioned that Pete was going to choose one of the homes he viewed to purchase immediately. He was short on time, needing to find a place quick so he could make the move for his job. It didn't get much easier than having a sale after only one day of parading around a client.

She had carefully lined up house after house to take him

to, according to his specifications. There were ten in all. He was looking for something in the suburbs, nothing too big since it was only him that would live there, but it had to have a fenced-in yard. Pete was a pet owner who wanted space for his dogs to play outside.

They had agreed to meet at Haylee's office because she was already going to be there gathering materials for him. She had printed handouts outlining the details of each home for him and had prepared as much of the paperwork for the offer as possible. The appointments were all set, and she had obtained all the codes for the lockboxes to retrieve the homes' keys.

When she had gotten up to leave, Scott was fast asleep in a mound of blankets. She was sorry she had to leave him. It would have been nice to sleep in or even just lie there beside him and be lazy. But she had bills to think about, and today there was a guaranteed paycheck at the end of the day. Technically, the check would not arrive for a few weeks until they closed the transaction, but typically for her, securing an accepted offer meant a done deal.

Pete arrived promptly, ten minutes before the time they scheduled to meet. As he walked up to shake her hand, Haylee was struck by how handsome he was. He had sandy blonde hair, bright piercing blue eyes the color of the ocean, and a toned, lanky build. He was just an inch or two taller than her. There was a small scar on his forehead that only seemed to add character. Dressed comfortably in khakis and a polo shirt, his smile was wide and easy as he stood in front of Haylee.

Haylee invited him to ride in her car. She usually offered to chauffeur her clients for showings. Most declined, insisting upon driving separate, but Pete gladly accepted. At times it was uncomfortable when she was stuck in a vehicle with someone she had nothing in common with, nothing to talk about. Fortunately, Pete and Haylee succeeded in keeping the dialogue rolling.

Haylee learned that Pete was looking forward to the location change because he had been sick of the Arizona weather. The temperature was consistently high, minus the humidity, so he figured the heat would be tolerable. He couldn't disagree more. The three years he had spent there had been enough, and he was ready for snowy winters and sticky summers.

Pete had been a finance major in college and had been employed in a bank since graduation. He started as a teller, working his way to branch manager, and then had requested to be transferred to a different location. He aspired to move as far up the chain as possible. Numbers had always been his thing.

Although he proclaimed himself as a bookworm, Haylee would never have guessed it. He was outgoing and personable, and the way he joked with her suggested he had a great sense of humor. She felt guilty that she assumed he would be pretentious because of his looks.

As she followed Pete while he casually strolled through the available homes, she had to remind herself that she was working. She tried to give Pete as much pertinent information as possible when they weren't gabbing about something totally unrelated.

By the time they were halfway through the houses on the list, Haylee had to admit that she thoroughly enjoyed Pete's company. She could see the two of them becoming good friends.

Any of the homes thus far could have worked for Pete, but when they reached the seventh house on the list, he was decided.

It had the prerequisite fenced yard with enough room for his dogs to move about. He could see himself spending plenty of evenings sitting out on the shaded wood deck lining the rear of the home. Although three bedrooms were not necessary, he figured he could occupy the master suite and use the other two as an office and a guest room.

The floor plan was open, without many walls separating the space. The house was only eight years old, the lighting fixtures had been updated, and the appliances all looked fresh out of the showroom. The colors on the walls were neutral and suited his tastes well, which was great because he did not want to have to fuss with much painting.

The one exception was the bedroom that had obviously been occupied by the young girl of the house. The bedroom was a bright pink, and little butterflies were stenciled on the wall. A plastic rainbow covered the light switch, and the dome covering the overhead bulb was a translucent rainbow to match. Pete could imagine the mockery he would endure if he didn't get it painted and changed right away. He supposed one out of eight rooms wasn't bad.

Haylee had seen the frown that came over Pete's face when she had flipped the rainbow switch. "Paint can be changed easily," she reminded him.

He couldn't help but sigh. "I know." He chuckled. "I think we have a winner here."

"Really? Great! Do you want to look at the rest on the list before deciding?"

Pete shook his head. "No need. This one will work. I actually really like it. Let's make an offer and be done with it."

Haylee couldn't be happier. Needless to say, the process wasn't always this simplistic. She certainly appreciated the fact that he didn't want to keep browsing when he had already made his choice.

"Well then, we can make the offer when you are ready. Today if need be."

He was anxious to get the ball rolling. "If you have time, I would like to get that done now." Pete glanced around the living room, mentally placing his furniture. "I'm hungry," he told her matter-of-factly. "Do you want to get some lunch while we work on the offer?"

After ignoring her growling stomach for the past hour, she was glad to oblige. "Sure. I missed out on breakfast this morning."

They decided to grab a quick sandwich at a café that had wireless Internet. That way, Haylee could do the market research on the home Pete chose while they waited for their food. He insisted that lunch was his treat, as a thank you to Haylee for her good work.

The investigation was easy due to the similarity of all the houses in the community. She determined the property was appropriately priced, but believed Pete could offer an amount with a few thousand shaved off the asking price.

"It is common for first time homebuyers to ask for closing cost assistance. We could add that dollar amount in the offer. But I will tell you that will make the sellers less likely to accept your lower priced offer."

With his financing secured, Pete knew how much he needed for closing costs and had that money set aside. "No need. I'd rather be sure they will take the offer."

Haylee drew a circle in the blank for a zero. "I think they will. If and when they do, we'll need to set up an inspection of the home. That way you can be certain there aren't any major defects."

"Do I need to find someone to do that?"

Haylee waved her hand through the air. "No. I can recommend a company for you. I use them a lot and have never had any problems. I'll attend the inspection too since you will be out of town again."

"That would be great. I'd probably drive the inspector nuts with a million questions."

She laughed. "You wouldn't be the only one, trust me. It's a big purchase and people want to know every little thing that might be wrong with it."

"Well I trust you'll know what to look for. I have to admit that I'm a total novice here. I know just enough to be dangerous."

Haylee appreciated the boost of confidence in his confession. One reason she liked her work was that she knew she helped people that might otherwise be lost without her.

"You'll be happy. Everything should go smoothly."

Pete crossed his fingers. "I hope so. I have a room at an extended-stay hotel starting next weekend. I don't want to be there too long. It gets expensive."

"Sounds like you've done it before. You move often?"

"I've done it once before. Only, that time I wasn't buying a house."

She joked, "Are you going to be here long enough to see a return on your investment?"

"The investment is my motivation. I want to have a reason to stay, to keep me planted in one place."

Haylee thoughtfully twirled her straw around in the cup of her iced tea. She had often wanted to be more of a jetsetter, change things up whenever she felt the need. It didn't happen that way for her. The career she selected would never get anywhere if she kept changing locales. Building a client base would be very difficult not knowing people in the area. She had to choose one over the other and make the sacrifice.

Pete continued, "I've wanted to live many different places. I guess I just like to try new things. I studied abroad every summer, somehow scraping money together while also using student loans. But now, I went where work took me, and I want to dig in deep."

"I bet that was exciting. Was it hard to meet people in different countries?"

"No. I still keep in touch with several of the friends I made. If I want to travel to those places, I have free room and board. Makes for a cheap vacation."

"I'll say. You have quite the network."

"Thank goodness for the Internet and e-mail. Otherwise, I wouldn't be able to afford my phone bill."

Pete checked his watch, reluctantly learning he had to get moving. "I hate to rush, but I have a plane to catch soon."

Haylee tossed the napkin in her hand on her plate before grabbing her purse. "No problem. I'll take you back to your car. I need to get your paperwork faxed anyhow."

When they pulled into the parking lot of Haylee's office, Pete was still working up his courage. Haylee's charm and enduring personality had drawn him in. And it didn't hurt that he found her very attractive. She had been proficient in her work, yet still forthcoming and amiable. Although he had noticed she didn't wear a ring on her left hand, he still worried she was taken. He couldn't see how she wouldn't be.

He timidly broached the subject he had been avoiding. He began, "Thanks for spending your Saturday showing me around, and helping me find a place. I had a good time today. I'll be back in two weeks, but call me when you have an answer on the offer. Or whenever you need to for that matter."

Pausing, he added, "Would you like to go out for dinner sometime? When I get back in town, that is."

She hadn't expected the question, and now realized that in all their chatter, Scott hadn't been mentioned.

Pete didn't take the hesitation as a good sign. He continued, "Or would it be inappropriate since I'm a client of yours?" He was inadvertently leading her toward an excuse. No one likes to be flat-out turned down.

She snapped back from her thoughts. "It's not so much that. I mean, yeah, its best to keep business and pleasure separate. But I um, I'm seeing someone."

He had guessed correctly, but was still quite disappointed. "Oh, I see…" he threw the strap of his briefcase over his shoulder, somehow comforted by her reason nonetheless. "It figures, all the good ones are taken."

Haylee was flattered by the comment. "I appreciate the offer. I could still introduce you to some people here if that's acceptable."

In her head, she instantly thought it was a dumb offer. Hadn't they just talked about all the friends he has everywhere? He obviously didn't have a problem meeting people. But they had been so in tune with each other that she thought it would be a shame if they weren't friends. Maybe he would be amenable with the alternative, even though she knew plenty of guys wouldn't be.

"Sure, that would be great." Not exactly his preference, but he was used to that. It was like the women say: always a bridesmaid, never the bride. Except he tended to be the 'friend' instead of the 'boyfriend'.

As an automatic, perfunctory gesture, Pete extended his hand for Haylee to shake. "Thanks again. We'll be in touch."

"No problem," she responded, as he gave her one last smile before disappearing into the driver's seat of his rental car.

Haylee was pleased how smoothly the transaction progressed. Within three days, she had an accepted offer from the sellers. To her chagrin, they hadn't sent her a counter offer, only a signed copy of what she had already sent. Haylee always expected to encounter some resistance in the form of negotiation, but the other realtor told her that his clients were extremely motivated because their old house was vacant. They were currently making double mortgage payments. Plus, Pete's offer was solid, and only slightly lower than what they asked for.

The inspection itself proved to be painless, with the exception that she had to wait a week and a half before an appointment was available. Haylee attended as promised. Some normal wear and tear was found, nothing out of the ordinary. She suggested Pete ask for a couple hundred dollars from the owners since the inspector had noticed a few thermal window seals had been broken and would need replaced. It wasn't a deal breaker, but she didn't think Pete should foot the bill for them. Since it was the only item on the inspection response, the sellers agreed quickly.

The closing date was set for the following Friday, so Pete would only have to stay at the hotel for a week. Haylee spoke with him several times over the phone to relay details of the sale to him. In fact, she was pretty sure they spoke almost daily for one reason or another. Either she had information to give him, or he had a question for her.

Pete's easygoing nature was a welcome, sharp contrast to Scott's dictatorial behavior. Since he had moved in, Scott had been more demanding than she had ever seen him. He wanted items moved, he needed things he couldn't find, and Haylee had dealt with the brunt of his temper. He had expressed what a pain in the ass he thought moving was, so Haylee chalked his grouchiness up to moving pains.

They had argued about furniture placement, decorations,

and, of course, closet space. Luckily, it was easy for Haylee to make space in her closet for Scott's clothes, but it was the other closets needed for storage that had been the problem.

Haylee put up a fierce resistance when Scott's old, beat-up recliner tried to make its way in her living room. It looked as though it had been in use since the turn of the century, and there wasn't enough room to squeeze it in. Scott argued that it was a very comfortable piece of furniture they could make space for. Haylee conceded when Scott placed it in a corner without moving anything else, but she already had plans of purchasing a cover for it. Or maybe he would just come home one day to find it mysteriously missing.

And to top her frustration, he was messy. Boxes were strewn around the house half unpacked, while clothes did not seem to find the hamper. Haylee had never considered how infuriating it would be to have cleaned a bathroom sink one day, only to find it peppered with shaven facial hair the next. She herself was not immaculate by any means, but a certain amount of hygiene *was* expected.

At the risk of sounding like a broken record, Haylee asked Scott to help her with some tidying up. While Scott stood in the hall bath that he now claimed as his, he surveyed the space. He took down the flower shaped hooks that hung the shower curtain with the same purple lilacs, replacing it with the plain, dark green curtain he had. He slung one of his black towels on the rack and stuffed the rest in the small closet beside the sink. The soap dish, toothbrush holder, wastebasket, and drinking glass all adorned the same pattern of flowers, so he collected them all and set them at the bottom of the closet. The walls were a subtle cream color, and he could live with that. He shoved his razor, deodorant, and toothpaste in the one available drawer.

Peering in, Haylee stood in the doorway noting the transformation.

"Making yourself at home?" she asked.

Scott obligingly emptied the last few items in the box he held. "You really didn't expect me to shower and shave surrounded by purple flowers did you?"

"Why not? It would show that you are comfortable in your manhood."

"No, it would prove that I was a pansy denying my true sexuality."

Her eyes rolled at his retort. When he offered to occupy the other bathroom, she had figured he would do some rearranging and couldn't blame him. But he wouldn't get by altering the work she had put in decorating without a little mockery.

"Anyway, I rearranged my stuff in the spare closet, if you want to use it for storage. Now you can bring your bike and golf clubs over."

By then he had moved into the bedroom to put away a box of clothes he had yet to empty, barely hearing what she had said. "Okay, thanks."

Not wanting to distract him from what she had been begging him to do, Haylee went out on her balcony to get some fresh air. A squirrel was startled by the opening of the sliding door and jumped to the adjacent tree branch that hung over the wood railing. Haylee watched as he scurried across the bare branches of the oak that had yet to bloom. The breeze outside was warm for this early in the year, and Haylee thought she could still smell the snow that had melted the prior day.

The patio furniture on her balcony was tall enough to clear the ledge, providing an unobstructed view. Made of wrought iron, the chairs came with red, padded seat covers, and the table had a glass top that was easy to clean. When the weather was warmer, she enjoyed eating meals out here. With the bustle below, she had company even when she dined alone.

Her mind began to drift, but was interrupted by the ringing of the cell phone in her pocket. She assumed it would be a client. Oftentimes she was called in the evenings.

But her guess proved incorrect when she saw it was Kathy's number. She had been meaning to call her, but hadn't had a chance since they went to the casino.

"Hey what's up?" was her greeting.

"Not much. I wanted to see how you were. Haven't talked to you for awhile."

"Oh. Good….same old."

"Scott getting settled in yet?"

"Getting there. He's putting clothes away right now. It's been an adjustment….but a good one."

When Haylee was done venting about her house being a mess, Kathy asked her, "Why aren't you speaking with Wendy?"

Since Wendy's allegation, Haylee had not taken any of her calls. She was still sore about the situation and didn't understand why Wendy had made such claims. She thought an apology was in order, but the voicemails she had from Wendy didn't hint at anything of the sort.

There was a long pause as Haylee bit her lip and contemplated how to answer. Kathy broke the silence. "Are you angry with her?"

Anger was not a frequent indulgence in her life. On the contrary, she steered clear of it. But this instance called for an exception in her eyes. "Yes."

"About what happened the other week?" Secrets amongst a group of friends were not easy to keep, and Kathy had pried it out of Wendy.

Haylee was instantly on the defense. "It didn't go as she

said. She took it all the wrong way, making a big deal out of nothing."

"Do you really think Wendy would just flat-out lie to you?" After spending time with him, Kathy was willing to believe what Wendy said and her take on the circumstances. Scott was pretending to be someone else when around Haylee. And Kathy was willing to bet it was a lot worse than just hitting on a friend once. It would amaze her if he wasn't already cheating.

"I'll admit that I wouldn't expect it from her, but Scott wouldn't lie to me. You should have seen the look on his face when I asked. He was shocked at the accusation."

Because she did not want to be alienated like Wendy, Kathy kept her opinions of Scott to herself. They were only opinions after all.

"If Wendy got the wrong impression, you two should talk and set it straight. Work it out." She was carefully avoiding taking sides, only mediating.

"When she takes it back and admits that she didn't know what she was talking about, maybe I will. An apology is due on her end."

Haylee made it obvious she was not going to take the first step toward a resolution. Kathy thought it a shame when a long-standing friendship was ruined over a misunderstanding. Wendy had been a good mutual friend of theirs since they met her a few years ago. But there wasn't much she thought she could do.

She sighed before answering, unwilling to argue with her. Wendy was not going to relent or go back on what she said. "Just try to talk to her when you can."

The conversation left a sour taste in Haylee's mouth when she hung up a few minutes later. While she fought back tears, the phone landed on the patio table with a slam. It was upsetting that Wendy was spreading this rumor of hers. She didn't want her friends to have the wrong impression.

Uncertainty was creeping back even though she had sworn it off. She reminded herself that Scott just had moved in, a testament to his commitment. He would not abandon her for someone else.

From behind her, Scott heard sniffles and watched as Haylee brushed a tear away from her face. He couldn't imagine what the commotion was or what had happened in the last fifteen minutes to provoke such a mood swing.

"What's the matter?" was all he could muster.

"Nothing…..I mean," she sniffled, "Are you sure you told me the truth? Nothing happened with Wendy?" She wanted to double-check with him once more to be certain.

He was sorry he asked. He had covered this with her already and had thought he was in the clear. What did it take to convince her? To the point, he answered, "YES. I'm sure." Patience was not his strong suit.

"Really?"

"*Really.*"

"Okay. Look I'm sorry, it's just that Wendy hasn't changed her story, and trust has always been hard for me. I DO believe you."

"Wendy is a fucking liar. Don't ask me what her problem is. Maybe she has a thing for me."

Haylee sat silent, staring at her feet as she contemplated the motive behind Wendy's story. It wasn't easy, nor fair, to be hearing two completely different stories, and she swallowed hard as her stomach turned over. Girls could be catty, she knew, and Scott showed no sign of changing his account. Her life was building around this man and it was only right to take his side and trust him.

Scott bent down to be eye level with Haylee. He lifted

her chin so their eyes could meet. "Can you please believe me so we can drop this?"

Haylee agreed to drop it. Wanting to dull the emotions that churned inside, she went to her bathroom and filled her tub with hot water, streaming lavender scented soap under the faucet that quickly created a wealth of bubbles. She slipped in, leaned her head against the rim of the tub and closed her eyes.

Chapter 13

The pulsating headache that had formed at the base of Haylee's neck the next morning only increased when Scott arrived home early from work. She was lost in thought in front of her computer in her home office, working on the monthly newsletter she sent to her mailing list of family, friends, and past and present clients. The template for the note was saved to her desktop, so after spending the morning at a neighbor's house filling out listing sheets, she went back home.

She almost panicked when she heard the front door open—she was more jumpy since she had been attacked. Relieved to see it was Scott, her muscles relaxed.

When he got closer, it was easy to see something was wrong. His face was sullen, and he was dropping the items he carried with loud thuds. It was still midday, and he hadn't mentioned leaving early. Normally he wasn't home until around six.

He slung his brown sport coat over the sofa on his way to the refrigerator. Scott decided on the way home that it wouldn't be a big deal if he woke up with a hangover tomorrow. He didn't have anywhere to be.

The first long swig destroyed half the bottle of cold lager. Wiping a few drops off his lips, he shook his head as he replayed the afternoon in his head. Bastards, was all he could think.

Haylee wandered in with an eyebrow raised. "Didn't expect to see you so early."

He finished off the first beer before responding. "Yeah, well, I figured it's a good day to come home and have a few beers. Why don't we go out for awhile tonight?"

"I guess we could. But not for too long, I have to be at the office at eight." She assumed that would be fine with him since he left earlier in the morning than she did. Confused, she asked, "Are we celebrating?"

Considering, he told her, "Um, something like that."

"Something like that? Or not that?"

He had already come up with the account he was going to give, candidly glossing over a few details. "I get to take a little extended vacation."

"Oh? What exactly does that mean?"

There wasn't an easy way to say it. She was going to be pissed. "Meaning I don't have to go to work tomorrow. Or the next day.....or until I find a new job."

Haylee's head was spinning. "You quit?"

"More like was let go…" he trailed off.

"You were fired?!"

"It was all bullshit really. They didn't give me a chance to explain. Some girl in my department claims I acted inappropriately, not doing my job right, and my boss calls me into his office and says he has to terminate my employment effective immediately." He technically called it sexual harassment, but Scott left that part out.

Haylee did not put two and two together. "Were you slacking off?"

Scott grunted. "My performance was not up to par." What a great way to put it, he thought. And not at all a lie.

He had made the mistake of getting too gracious with Susan, one of his immediate supervisors. Evidently, he mistook her flirty behavior for advances when really she was only trying to be friendly. She didn't take too well to his propositions, and complained to their region's manager. Unfortunately for Scott, Susan carries a lot of weight with the company executives.

Haylee asked, "Is there no recourse? Can they just do that to you?"

"Sure they can. I didn't have any kind of contract with them binding my employment. My employers can basically do whatever they want."

It was a bleak thought and a disagreeable situation at best. Haylee was not keen on the idea of having an unemployed 'roommate'. Scott had yet to pay her back for the casino outing, or give her the promised advanced rent. They had agreed he would help her with the mortgage and utilities and to split entertainment and food costs. But *her* checkbook was taking the most hits.

"What about the bills? What are you going to do?"

The cap on his second beer twisted off easily and let out a hiss of carbonation. "I'll find something else. I'm not too worried about it. Besides, you paid all the bills before I got here so we can manage for the time being can't we?" She reluctantly nodded. "I obviously didn't anticipate getting canned, but it's not like it will remain that way. Things happen, I can't change that."

Scott genuinely didn't want to get fired, but if it was in his cards, it couldn't have happened at a better time.

Haylee was there to help, whereas if he still lived with his old roommate, he would have been screwed. He didn't do a whole lot of saving, most of his paychecks disappeared almost as quickly as they were given. So before, to be without an income was to be without any living expenses. He could imagine the humiliation of having to ask to borrow money. But Haylee was the one that said she didn't want them to keep score with one another and fight about who paid for what.

"I take back saying we could go out. I think its best if we stay in and not spend a bunch of money until you find something new." At a very minimum, she thought.

Scott sighed as he propped himself up on the kitchen counter. "I suppose you are right." He would have much rather she said that she didn't give a hoot, but that was probably asking too much. Extending his arms, he told her, "Now come over here and give me some sympathy. I've had a rough day."

She did as asked. Haylee portrayed a sympathetic mate, but inside she was a fit of rage. She had a hard time understanding how he could be so calm and collected about the situation. She would be a mess.

It appeared to her that Scott's sense of responsibility didn't run as deep as her own. It was a major difference between the two of them, one she could see causing conflict. But then again, maybe she overcompensated her accountability more than anyone else. Scott included. She would need time to cool off before she made any conclusions.

One thing she knew for sure. The timing of this incident sucked.

Pete sat next to Haylee at the closing. It was obvious to him that something was bothering her because she did not have her usual pep. Although, it was eight a.m., and she had mentioned before that she was not much of a morning person. The large mug of steaming coffee placed on the table in front of her was sure to remedy the sleepy fog that may hang over her head.

The dark circles under her eyes told him that she had not slept much the night before, for whatever reason. Maybe she was out late, having a good time. He was curious, but didn't ask.

They sat at a long wood table that stretched several feet. Besides them, it accompanied the middle-aged couple selling their house, their rosy cheek realtor of the same age who wore her hair in a tight bun, and at the head of the table was their closing agent, Ted, from the title company. He was closer to Haylee and Pete's age, perhaps even a few years younger. The thick stack of papers he was shuffling around threatened to collapse on the floor if he wasn't careful with them. A pencil was stuck over one ear and his face was wrinkled with stress as he continued to separate the documents into a 'seller' and 'buyer' pile. End-of-the-month closings were popular and numerous, and one look at the closing agent confirmed it. Pete could picture him pulling balls of hair out of his head behind closed doors while in between clients.

Pete's hand ached and cramped as he signed endless paperwork. He couldn't believe how many t's had to be crossed and how many i's there were to be dotted. Disclosures, affidavits, and insurance forms stacked a half-inch thick had awaited his signature. Haylee told him to be thankful he hadn't needed a second mortgage or else the same stack would have been doubled. God forbid each loan package not be separate.

After attempting to read two or three documents in their entirety, Pete heeded Haylee's advice to listen to the closer's explanation and summary of what he was signing. They would be there forever if he kept trying to read all the fine print. Haylee promised him that many people in her office used that particular title company and there had never been any problems. They wouldn't pull a fast one on him where he unknowingly signed his life away.

When Ted confirmed that the loan transfer was complete and all paperwork had been filled out, he congratulated the couple on the sale and Pete on being a homeowner.

Pete took a moment to shake hands with everyone at the table, thanked them, and then turned to Haylee.

"One last thanks to you for helping me get this together so quickly."

The envelope in her hand containing the commission check was all the thanks she technically needed, but verbal gratitude was always welcome. "Anytime. If people you know are as decisive and simplistic in their needs as you are, please send them my way," she joked. "Okay, even if they aren't, send them my way. I would be happy to help."

His schedule was clear to allow for moving and unpacking, but he wasn't ready to get to it. He snatched a chocolate chip cookie off the tray of the nearby refreshment stand, hardly a substitute for the breakfast he had missed. "Want to go grab some coffee? You didn't get to finish that mug they gave you."

Awake until four in the morning, Haylee had slept until her alarm went off. She then proceeded to fall back asleep almost as fast as she had turned the alarm off. She had scrambled to get herself together before leaving the house, not even having time to make a coffee to go. Plus, she had already resolved to take it easy that day since she was working the weekend.

"I could use about four more cups. There's a place less than a block down."

Outside, the sun was especially bright, and Haylee squinted until she dug her sunglasses out of her purse. The days were increasingly getting warmer as spring approached, but trees had yet to show any signs of blooming. Birds were still hiding out down south and yards had not yet been mowed. Spring lingered just a short stretch into the distance, but for now, the promise of its approach was enough. Pete and Haylee began their short walk after Haylee had pulled her jacket over her shoulders.

While Pete babbled about his new place, Haylee strolled silently beside him, lost in thought, her eyes on the ground. She could remember when she was young and wouldn't step on the cracks in the sidewalk. It was a game she liked to play with anyone that would participate, and she'd show them how you had to jump the divots like they were three-foot-high hurdles. It used to be so easy to keep herself amused.

Seeing her smirk, Pete asked, "What's funny? I didn't think you were going to smile all day."

In truth, Haylee had no idea she had been that transparent. When things were bothering her, she usually covered it up pretty well. "Nothing. It's silly…I used to make a game out of the breaks in the sidewalk. Thinking of it made me laugh."

"Good game."

"Yeah…wait, huh? Are you teasing me?"

"No. I used to do the same thing. My parents started it. They would lift me by my arms and swing me over them. Later on, I'd pull at their arms so I could jump higher."

"You're kidding," Haylee alleged.

"Nope. We had all sorts of games. I think they tried to always entertain me. We traveled a lot, and there weren't any other children to keep me occupied."

"Oh. So, was it just the three of you?"

"Yep. My mother has diabetes and I was a high-risk

pregnancy. She got lucky and didn't want to chance it again."

Pete had wanted siblings for several years when he was young, but then had become accustomed to his small family. Because of it, he had a very close bond with each of his parents. They had not only shown *him* love, but to this day, shown him what it meant to be *in* love in a marriage. He wanted to have what they had.

Haylee nodded in understanding. It was one more aspect they had in common. But Haylee didn't want to get into a conversation right now about childhood, so she didn't say anything. The timing was perfect regardless, they were at their destination.

"This is it," Haylee told him, and pointed toward the door.

Pete pulled the glass door open, waiting behind it while Haylee walked through. The gush of warm air that rushed toward him as he walked in had the chill he collected from the walk trickling away. The aroma from the fresh baked goods behind the shop's counter had Pete's stomach instantly growling, so he was happy there wasn't a long line in front of them.

The young woman behind the cash register wore a white apron and a baseball cap sporting the store's logo. Her name tag read 'Julie'. She politely asked, "What can I get for you today?"

Unlike Pete, Haylee had smelled nothing but coffee beans when they came in. "Just black coffee please. Large," she added.

Julie pressed a few buttons on the register before she looked up. "And you?" she asked as she glanced over to Pete.

"I'll have the same, but with plenty of room for cream.

And one of those blueberry muffins you have in the case here," Pete told her as he pointed it out.

She plucked a piece of wax paper from a box before reaching in to grab Pete's muffin. "They are still very warm," she said. "Do you want butter for it?"

"Sure," he said. He looked at Haylee. "Are you sure you don't want anything to eat?"

She had been examining the display in front of her. "Actually yeah, can I get that yogurt parfait as well?" she inquired to Julie.

Haylee gathered her coffee and yogurt after it was placed on the counter.

"Eleven fifty," Julie declared after she punched in the yogurt to the order.

Simultaneously, they both said, "I'll get it."

Pete laughed. "Great minds think alike." He put the twenty dollar bill he already had out into Julie's hand. "I was faster. Why don't you grab us a seat?"

Haylee obliged, snatching a few sugar packets from the condiment stand on her way over. She tried to expel the thoughts that centered on her frustrations with Scott before Pete came over, but didn't succeed.

Her brow was furrowed as she stared into her cup. When he was seated in front of her, Pete asked, "Are you alright today?"

Haylee was not one to divulge personal business to clients. Yet somehow, she was having trouble seeing Pete as merely a client.

"I'm fine. I was just up late last night." A yawn stifled out as if to prove her statement. "I'm a worrier. If I get too much on my mind, I'll stare at the ceiling only wishing for sleep."

Pete finished chewing the bite of moist, buttery muffin he had anxiously stuffed in his mouth. "I think we all do that from time to time. What's got you going? Is it at least going to be resolved soon?"

Haylee paused before answering. "Not exactly. The time frame is, well, undetermined."

"Is it work-related?" he probed.

"No. Personal-related. Roommate issues you could say."

"I see," Pete said before sipping his coffee. "Let me guess….she won't stop stealing your shoes?" He grinned foolishly as he said it.

"No. *He* has no interest in taking my shoes or clothing. It's a totally different issue."

"Ahh." Pete didn't think for one minute the problem would be as simplistic as his 'guess'. But he also hadn't presumed her roommate would be male. It was clear to him now that she was talking about her significant other. And if he had her this upset, he didn't fathom himself being an objective sounding board for her.

"I suppose I just have lived on my own for too long," she claimed, though she didn't quite believe it.

"It would be an adjustment then." He could remember when he lived with a past girlfriend. There had been plenty of issues for them to sort out. Unfortunately, no matter how accommodating either one of them had been, it flat-out didn't work. They had come to a mutual agreement that they weren't compatible and had parted ways graciously.

He decided not to share that information. "You'll work things out," he assured her. Though for his own selfish reasons, he wouldn't be upset if they didn't. She was more attractive to him, not just physically but also mentally, each time he saw her.

Haylee slowly shook her head in agreement while she poked at her parfait. It was reassuring that Pete was so positive, but then, she couldn't remember any instances where he was otherwise. He was like a rock. She imagined that no matter how nervous, he wouldn't shake and crumble, nor would he cower in a corner when depressed. If he was angry, no fists or inanimate objects would be thrown. He was steady, solid, consistent, never going to the extremes, and all without being boring.

She didn't have enough people like that in her life.

If her mind had a volume, Pete would have been able to hear the wheels turning within it. He waited patiently while she deliberated.

Sensing her own detachment, Haylee snapped back. "So, you have a lot to do today. Don't you need to get started on unpacking?"

"I have all weekend. I'll get it done. It's getting motivated to get started that is hard."

Haylee took the final swig of coffee. "Don't let me keep you."

He would let her keep him all day. "You're not. But you may want to run out of here before I try to recruit you for help."

Despite any guilt that might result, she didn't want to leave Pete's company yet. "That would depend. What kind of help?"

"Do you like to paint?"

"I don't mind it."

"Great, because I can't stand to do so. I bought a nice shade of masculine blue to cover up all the pink in the spare bedroom. I want to get the painting done before I shove a bunch of stuff in there."

Haylee clucked her tongue. "What? You aren't going to leave those cute butterflies on the wall? What's wrong with you? You are going to ruin all that artistry."

Pete narrowed his eyes at her. "As good as it is, I would never hear the end of it if I left it. That will be my spare bedroom, and you don't know some of my friends. They want to visit soon, and will have to stay in that room. I would get a new nickname like 'Pinky' or 'Fairy'," he professed. "No thanks."

She pictured some burly guys pointing and laughing with Pete as their object of ridicule, and was entertained by the thought. "Well, we wouldn't want that. Let's get right on changing it."

"Really? I wouldn't, by any means, expect your help. I'm sure you have plenty of work to do."

"That's the beauty of my job. I have no set schedule," she stated. "And since you made the transaction so simple, I'll volunteer some brushstrokes to make it easier on you."

Pete clapped his hands together. "Alright. I can't really turn down help, seeing as though I don't have much of it. Do you need to change?"

She had dressed more casually since it was a Friday. "I have a T-shirt in the car I can throw on when we get to the house. Your house," she corrected.

"My house," he echoed. "I like the sound of it."

Chapter 14

$\mathcal{H}$aylee drove to Pete's new place lost in her thoughts. The car windows were rolled down, and as the wind came through to tousle her hair, she hoped it would also blow away her troubles. It was easy to remember the days, not long ago, when all she had to worry about was herself. As selfish as that may be, it had worked for her well. She had always cared a great deal about family and friends, and had shown her generous side to them often. But when it came down to making her life work, she had only needed to rely on herself. Now, she had someone else in her life that contributed to maintaining that balance. And at the moment, he was completely throwing that balance off.

He was a major determinant of Haylee's frame of mind. And with things such as the recent job loss, it affected Haylee's disposition in a powerful way. What he did and didn't do right became a small obsession for her to dwell on. But what bothered her most was the control was out of her hands and there was nothing she could do about it.

Control. It may be the single most important driving

factor for her. She had sought to maintain rule over her own domain, without interference. Her subconscious must have done its job by urging her to remain alone. Now that she broke that trend, the tenacious part of her believed the pair could happily make it work. And that in turn led to a weakness of hers, that when most would give up, she instead kept on pushing. Kept on insisting everything was alright. She hadn't truly been ready to face those demons, but now she was forced to do so.

When she came upon a gas station, Haylee pulled in for gas and a soda. She hissed at the pump as she finished, eyeing the total it read. If these prices kept up, she would have to start charging a fee to drive her clients around.

Entering the store, she strolled past the coolers and decided on a diet cola. When she turned to start for the counter, Wendy was in her path.

Startled, cursing to herself because there was no way to avoid her or pretend she didn't see her, Haylee didn't know what to say. After a brief silence, Wendy spoke.

"Hi, how've you been?" Wendy had seen her come in and purposely confronted her. She was hurt, but was also determined to rectify the state of affairs.

Scowling at her, yet somewhat embarrassed, she replied, "Just fine thanks." Sidestepping Wendy she said, "Excuse me."

Wendy grabbed her arm before she could get past. "Will you just talk to me for a minute? Geez, I didn't want it to be this way, that you won't even talk to me."

Haylee turned on one heel. "How did you expect it to be? When a friend betrays me, I sit idly by and laugh about it? Well, you were mistaken."

Wendy had never seen this kind of temper in her friend. She didn't know Haylee had in it her. But her resentment was aimed at the wrong person. Even if their friendship wasn't strong enough to get past this debacle, Wendy wanted to try to make her understand.

She remained calm and suggested, "There is a bench outside. Let's go sit down."

Haylee struggled to be sensible in the midst of her feelings. She barked at her, "I need to go pay first."

When she finished, she dropped herself down across from Wendy. She was flabbergasted that she was finding it so easy to be callous. "Make it fast, I have somewhere to be."

Wendy wasn't one for conflict and had considered apologizing so they could just put the dispute behind them. But then she saw Sarah again, and instead opted for tough love.

"Alright. I know I have hurt your feelings but I didn't intend to. You told me once that you would rather know the truth then to be oblivious. So that is what I did for you. And unfortunately, I am going to do that for you again."

She paused, watching Haylee's eyes drill into her.

"Scott's friend Sarah told me to call her sometime so we could meet up for drinks, so I did. After having a few, Sarah became loose-lipped and let it slip that she and Scott have been sleeping together. Recently. She realized her mistake and asked me to keep it between us, but for your sake I wasn't going to."

The breath she had been inhaling was instantly knocked away from her. Haylee didn't know whether to slap Wendy's mouth shut, or to fall on her shoulder sobbing. She did neither.

When Haylee only stared at her, she continued.

"I care about you, and I don't want to see you be deceived by someone you love. You deserve better than that. I hope you understand that I don't want to be the bearer of bad news, but I thought you should find out sooner rather than later. We have been friends long enough that I would like to think you know I wouldn't lie to you about something like this."

Never having been faced with this dilemma before, Haylee couldn't discern how to respond. Her face went white. She could feel her lip tremble. She thought she might get sick.

She began to rise from her seat. "I have to go." She wanted to be alone, to think.

Wendy grabbed her wrist before she walked away. As frustrating as it was to not be trusted, it was even worse to be aware that someone was toying with Haylee's heart. "I know you probably don't believe me right now, but look into what I said."

Haylee jerked her arm away and headed to her vehicle. She fought back the sobs, biting her lip hard until she was safely inside, and then pulled into the street.

It didn't take long for the first tear to fall.

Pete was beginning to wonder if Haylee had changed her mind. He picked up his cell phone for the third time to see if he had missed a call from her, but no such luck. The movers were unloading the truck with Pete's belongings at a swift pace and the house was filling up quickly. He had made sure that his bed and sheets were unpacked first so that he had a place to sleep that night. The floor was such unappealing option.

Roxy and Champ, Pete's loyal companions, had happily explored their new territory outside and wore themselves out running around in the yard. Now each of them was curled up on old, oversized pillows, sleeping peacefully despite the noise. Pete looked at them enviously while he surveyed all the work yet to be done. He wanted to get his things put away as quickly as he could so that he could then investigate his new surroundings.

When the doorbell rang, Roxy and Champ bolted to the door while Pete followed. Haylee stood on the front porch, peering in through the open door, and was surprised when eight paws and two pink tongues began their assault on her. She bent down to give them the attention they were so greedily seeking out, but had to throw her head back a few times to avoid getting licked repeatedly in the face.

"You could have just come in since the door is open. They were sleeping so you could have avoided the attack if you hadn't rung the bell and woken them."

She rubbed Champ's head with one hand and Roxy's exposed belly with the other. "I don't mind, I actually like it. I didn't want to start roaming around your house without you. I figured you were busy unpacking in one of the rooms, so I rang the bell to get your attention."

He shook his head in amusement of the animals. "You would have thought they have never seen another person before, the way they act when they meet people." Pete noticed that Haylee's face was a little red, almost as if she had been crying.

Haylee had taken her time getting up to his front stoop. She was sure to check the mirror and dust more powder on her face to cover up the redness before she had exited her car. In truth, she was bewildered that she had continued to make her way to Pete's house without a second thought. But confronting Scott was not an option at the moment seeing as though he was not home, and all she really wanted to do was calm down.

Seeing Pete's face, and his dogs, was a good start.

"They are very affectionate," Haylee announced as she rose from her knees. She snickered out loud. "Although, when you said you had dogs, this isn't what I pictured." The two fluffy, white west highland terriers couldn't weigh more than twenty pounds each. "These are chick dogs. Not the big manly ones I had pictured."

Pete grinned. "Never mind. I don't need your help anymore."

Though she thought it impossible, Haylee smiled back. "Fine. I'll be going. Have fun painting," she told him despite the fact that she had no intention upon leaving to go face her dilemma.

He scooped the dogs up, one in each arm so that Haylee could get through the door. "No, no. I didn't mean it. Like I said, I won't turn away the help. Not even the kind that mocks me."

He motioned her to follow him and continued. "I had wanted a pet, but I kind of inherited these two. When my aunt passed away, no one in the family could take them in, and I couldn't bear taking them to a shelter. So I was their new home. They were confused at first, but they've adjusted."

She would have to agree by the way they obediently followed Pete's order to go in the kitchen to lie down. Happily, they each plopped down on their respective pillows. Pete put a gate up to keep them from getting into mischief while they painted.

He had already put tape around the trim in the room and had placed a tarp on the carpet to catch any splatter. Pete handed one brush to Haylee, and started to spread the first coat on the adjacent wall with another. The blue hue was dark, much more so than the pink on the wall, negating any need for primer. Haylee volunteered to get around the edges while Pete filled in the middle.

Pete could tell she was still troubled, but she was doing a good job of trying to cover it up.

Between the two of them, the first coat was finished fast. Haylee stood tall on the ladder to reach the last corner at the edge of the nine-foot ceiling. Descending down the rungs, Haylee's foot slipped in a clumsy motion. Struggling to keep her balance, the small container holding her paint toppled down the front of her while the ladder teetered and tottered. Hearing the commotion and Haylee's startled utterances, Pete went over and did his best to prevent her from slamming into the wall and potentially hurting herself. Haylee fell backward into Pete while everything else crashed to the floor.

Grounded now, Pete looked at a blue-checkered Haylee covered in paint. "Are you alright?"

She had no injuries to claim, with the exception of a stubbed toe. More humiliated than anything else, she apologized for the mess. "Oh my God, I am so sorry! I lost my footing. Look at this wreck! A lot of help I am."

The 'wreck' as she put it, merely consisted of Haylee's clothing and the tarp. "No big deal. That's why I put the tarp on the floor, just in case. I should be apologizing to you. You just lost those clothes on my account, they will never come clean."

She looked at the colorful spray adorning the pants and shirt she wore. She let out something between a laugh and a cry. "Did I mention that I'm a klutz?"

If she hadn't been so stressed out to begin with, it would have been easier to laugh it off. "Look, there's some on your shirt too from when you caught my fall."

To prove it wasn't the disaster she thought it was, he smeared the paint across his shirt, getting it all over his fingers, and then marked her nose. "There. Now the look is complete. Your face was lacking color."

Still poised in Pete's lap on the tarp, she relaxed at his easy reaction. "No fair." She proceeded to even the score, giving Pete reflection stripes as though he was a football player preparing for a game.

When he laughed, Haylee was reminded why she was so drawn to Pete's personality. And she couldn't deny that he was very good-looking. Their faces were so close that it would very easy to lean into him and let the magnetic pull take over.

In Pete's mind, Haylee fit well in his embrace. Even through the paint, he could smell the floral scent she had put on her neck that morning. It was enticing, drawing him nearer. He considered himself a courteous man, but was compelled to get to know her despite the knowledge he had of her situation.

Snapping the trance that had fallen over them, Haylee carefully began to rise. For the time being, her loyalty was still to Scott. "I need to get cleaned up. Do you have any soap out yet?"

He had no right to be, but Pete was disappointed. "I do, and I can find a shirt and sweats for you to change into. It won't be flattering, but at least you won't get paint all over your car."

"Would you grab a trash bag too? These clothes are old so I am going to throw them out. I don't want to deal with trying to get the stains out."

"Yeah, no problem."

Haylee stepped into the bathroom and closed the door behind her. Despite her uncertain state of affairs, she wasn't going to give Pete the idea that she was open to exploring a romantic relationship. Even if it turned out that Scott had done it to her, she wasn't going to be a cheater. She couldn't inflict that kind of hurt on someone, regardless of the circumstances. She had seen first-hand the damage it can cause.

Pete knocked, and Haylee cracked the door to get the items he had gathered. While she scrubbed her nose, she probed herself on why she was there in the first place. She told herself it was to do a client a favor, one who had turned into a friend. But she suspected that wasn't exactly the truth. It was deeper than that but she wasn't ready to admit it.

She could hear her phone ring in the other room, and decided that no matter who it was, she would use the call as an excuse to leave the situation.

She emerged with paint residue still clinging to her skin, regardless of her best efforts. Casually seeking out her cell, she brushed the wet hair from her face that had fallen over her eyes. While she listened to the voicemail, she furrowed her brow as though she was concentrating intently, focused on the message.

She returned the phone back to her purse and told Pete, "That was a client. I'm sorry, but I have to go."

In actuality, it was Scott yelling into the receiver, inquiring, no, demanding to know where she was. She had told him she would be at the office after the closing, and he had stopped by there to see her. The front desk told him they hadn't seen her all day.

"Urgent business?"

"Unfortunately. I'm 'on call' every day," she stated as she mused over Scott's impeccable timing.

"That would be a tough aspect of any job," he claimed. "But I understand." He took a few steps closer to her. "I am bummed to see you go."

With restraint on his part, Pete stepped closer to Haylee, settling for a lengthy hug and a kiss to her cheek. He lingered there longer than intended.

Her heart jumped into her throat and she felt a wave of heat wash over her. When he slowly pulled away, she glimpsed the affection in his eyes. It was hard just then to remember any reason to draw back, even harder to understand how her heart could be tugged in two very different directions.

Not knowing what else to do, she all but ran out the

door. "Bye," she called over her shoulder as she scurried toward her car. Now what was she going to do about that? she asked herself. Friendship with Pete was going to be very difficult, if not impossible.

Chapter 15

~~~~~~~~~~~~~~~~~~

*H*aylee began to feel quite alone. She had sorted through her thoughts, gathering enough courage to once again ask Scott about his endeavors. He did not take it well, and became angry. After saying he was sick of having discussions regarding his fidelity, he spent a few days not talking to her.

Imagine how you would feel being accused all the time, he had said. Not exactly the reaction she had expected, but she supposed it was warranted. She would not appreciate the finger always being pointed in her direction either.

After the third night of silence, Haylee caved. Even though what she believed changed every other day, hell, every other hour, she couldn't stand the tension between them and asked for a truce. They made up for an hour before falling asleep that night, but it didn't quite feel right to Haylee.

The activities that used to energize her were of little interest. Parties? No thanks. Chatting with friends over dinner? Pass. Work? How about the bare minimum. Though, she couldn't skimp as much as she wanted to since she really needed the income.

Patience was one of her strengths, but it was surely being tested. Three weeks had passed since Scott had become unemployed and there weren't any glimmers of a potential job prospect. He had been looking, she knew that for a fact since she had sat with him while he was online searching, but he wanted to be choosy. He refused to take just anything that came his way.

Truth be told, he was having a difficult time talking employers past the fact he had just been fired, but he didn't convey that to Haylee. Scott was enjoying the time off while he regrouped himself.

His visits with Sarah had ceased in light of her big mouth. She had apologized, but then laughed it off. She claimed that he belonged with her anyway, and she didn't doubt he would see that soon. But he wasn't as convinced. The two of them did have plenty in common, even the fact that they had a hard time staying committed to anyone. Scott wasn't sure he could handle being on the other side of the fence.

While he watched television that evening, Haylee sat beside him. He slipped his arm around her shoulder and she lowered her head down on his chest. Scott absently stroked his fingers through Haylee's hair.

Her muddled thoughts cleared some by the comfort of Scott's touch. She was able to focus then, becoming aware of the show they were watching. She had been too distracted to notice before.

His lips brushed her forehead, lazily planting a kiss before they left. She nuzzled in closer, embracing the warmth of his body. It was that comfort that had her refusing to let go of Scott, like a drug that crazed her. The drug could be found elsewhere, in more suitable places, but that knowledge eluded her. She didn't know any better.

"What do you want to do this weekend?" he asked her during a commercial.

"Not sure. I have to do open houses on Saturday and Sunday afternoon."

Confused, he said, "I thought those were only held on Sundays."

She let out one huffing sigh. "No. Sundays are most frequent, but it can be both. A listing I have really wants to get the ball rolling and get the extra exposure. I didn't have the heart to tell them that open houses almost never sell the house. Half the time it's just curious neighbors peeking in, or casual buyers."

"Casual buyers?"

"Yeah, those that are only looking to get ideas and who probably won't purchase for a year or two."

"Maybe you'll get lucky."

Her cynical side did the speaking. "Or maybe I'll be stuck doing them for three months every weekend until it sells. Better chance of that."

He could empathize. For as long as he had worked full time, the minute his watch hit five o'clock on Friday, he didn't even so much as think about work until Monday morning. Giving up that free time was never an option.

"Why don't you tell them you can't do it? You shouldn't be expected to work every day of the week. Or have someone else do them for you, one of the new agents. Don't you guys do that?"

"Yes we do, but to answer your first question, I just can't. My job is all about building relationships, and I can't very well do that if another agent is at their home all weekend. The idea is to put in my time now, so later I don't have to do it. Once you have impressed enough people, business typically comes to you through referrals. The workload may not lessen but it becomes easier in a way." She envisioned the team she would one day lead. "Assistants can take care of the aspects you don't want to deal with any longer."

The price tag it entailed was too high for him. He liked the end result she saw for herself, and the financial success that would come along with it, but the path was a very long dirt road. He would rather find a golden brick driveway that was a hop, skip, and jump away from the prize.

"Sounds like you'll be very busy. Who would play the role of Suzy Homemaker?"

She teased, "I suppose you could. In fact, we could start practicing right now seeing as though you aren't preoccupied. I could figure out some chores."

A shudder rippled through him when words like laundry and mopping came to mind. "Chores like eighteen holes of golf?"

"Fat chance of that. Dream on."

A sneer began to form at the corner of his lips. "Homemaker is not on my resume. I know you don't think I would end up as a Mr. Mom do you?"

A ball of pent of fury was knotting in her stomach. "If we are talking about a hypothetical future here, which I'll assume we are, I'll have you know that I am not some kind of miracle worker with a side talent of magic. I couldn't take care of everything."

Scott pulled away and put his back up against the arm of the couch to face her. "Okay. Well, hypothetically, how exactly would you define help?" He gestured with fingers to indicate that the word help was in quotations.

While her temper flared, her tolerance dwindled. "Splitting the housework. For example, I would clean the bathrooms while you vacuumed. Or taking turns feeding the kids. Taking the dog for a walk. Don't you think that is only fair?"

Dancing around the question, Scott told her, "Honey, housework, as you say, and I don't get along well. You *could* count on me to mow the lawn, but seeing as though right now we live in a condo where it's done for us, it isn't necessary. If you are copasetic with eating something out of a fast-food window for dinner, then maybe I could help you there. And kids? Geez, I don't even know that I want any, and I certainly don't want a pet."

Haylee's mouth hung gaping in shock. She stared at him as though he was from a different planet. Slowly shaking her head, she bit her lip in order to avoid exploding out.

Deep breaths, she thought. What cloud of ignorance had she been floating on to think they had the same opinions when it came to domestic matters? No kids or pets? Those two elements were big factors of what made a house a home in her opinion. She couldn't possibly live without that. She felt that a rosy veil had been ripped off her eyes to expose a nasty reality.

It was his immature perspective, she decided. He didn't understand it from a female's view. Well, she could help change that.

She diffused her anger so she could attempt a rational discussion.

"Why are you hesitant about having children?"

Her lack of anger spoke volumes to him about her tolerance of conflict. "I like my freedom, and that's a huge responsibility."

There was a click in Haylee's mind as her gears spun. Responsibility and freedom were the operative words Scott had used, and she could see how they were contributing to their problems.

"It *is* a huge responsibility, which makes it scary. But

the intangible rewards make it worth it." She believed his anxiety was getting the best of him. "And I'll help you and chores get along better."

Scott didn't see any reason to argue over things that may never become an issue. Haylee wasn't particularly scornful, but nonetheless, he didn't want to risk any unnecessary nagging about his outlook. "I'll bet you would. We'll just have to see."

Kathy was feeling determined. Weeks had passed since she had last seen Haylee, and she missed her. There had been times when she had called her, hoping for advice or an ear to listen, and e-mails had been sent asking her about weekend plans. But her attempts had gone unanswered or had been repeatedly turned down for one reason or another. But not today.

Excitement had filled her all day, with the latest development in her life. She couldn't wait to tell her closest friend that she was newly engaged. When Jake asked her the night before, she had been pleasantly surprised. Sure, it had been a fast courting period, but it was her belief that when you knew, you knew. So why wait?

It had been the best thing to happen to her. She threw herself down on her red, microfiber sofa, and with a dreamlike grin firmly in place, she popped the cork to the bottle of champagne she had picked up at the store on her way home. Now that her workday was over, she could finally pour herself a glass. She hoped Haylee would join her in the festivities since she had celebrated all last night with Jake.

She glanced at the old grandfather clock in her living room. It had been passed down through the generations of her family. Solid oak framed the roman numerals inside, with hands that were currently pointing toward five o'clock.

Usually Haylee went to the office earlier on Fridays so that she could make a timely exit at the end of the day. Betting she had left by now, Kathy dialed her number. She snarled in frustration and annoyance when the call went unanswered. Shortly after hanging up without leaving a message, she received a text message from Haylee saying she had not yet left the office, but it also asked what Kathy had needed.

Kathy responded back with her intentions of the call, inviting Haylee over for drinks and dinner. She even said she had something major to tell her. News of this sort needed to be conveyed in person, though it was about to burst out of her like a balloon that had been filled with too much water.

A few minutes passed before a response was finally made. Haylee explained she was already going to see a movie with Scott. She didn't even acknowledge the part about Kathy's news. Kathy waited several minutes to see if another message might be sent, but to no avail.

"Thanks a lot," Kathy said to the message her silver flip phone held. "Glad I could count on you."

Understanding of the situation eluded her. She had figured Haylee would at least be curious to hear what Kathy had to report. After all, she said it was major. She didn't fathom she had to send a message with the words 'urgent' or 'nine-one-one' to get a measly call back.

It crossed her mind to call again to bark out the information, even if she had to leave it on voicemail, but she refrained. If she wasn't worth the time, then Haylee wasn't worth the bother.

Haylee called out to her mother to announce that she was there. Seeing as though the visit was not arranged in advance, she did not want to walk in unexpectedly and frighten her. Her mother's house was on her way to the open house she was having that afternoon.

Diane called out in answer, claiming she would be out of the bathroom momentarily. After scooping up Peanut first for petting, Gizmo yipped insistently at her feet in jealousy. Peanut licked her face in welcome before she set him down to give Gizmo her chance. They knew the routine and followed Haylee to the jar where Diane kept their treats. She had them perform their tricks prior to handing out their snack. They greedily scooped up the biscuits before scurrying away to separate corners of the living room to enjoy them.

It was only ten thirty in the morning so Haylee assumed the coffee she smelled was still fairly fresh. Helping herself while she waited, she grumbled when she only found skim milk in the refrigerator.

Her Mom walked in, hair still dripping from the shower. She walked to where her daughter stood in order to hug her. "Where's those creamers you always have? I want something sweet."

Diane settled down at the round breakfast table, the view of her small, lush backyard in sight. She made a mental note to pick up mulch that day before she answered. "Oh. I ran out. Today is grocery day." She pulled the list that was already started on the table toward her. "But there is a blueberry danish left in the pantry that can satisfy your sweet tooth, if that will do for you."

"It would." When she was cranky, she often craved sugar. She hoped the funk would pass, or else it could mean trouble for her waistline. She didn't bother with a plate, only grabbing a napkin to put the pastry on.

The women jumped when the dogs began to bark out the sliding glass door, inches away from the table. Peering out, Haylee could see that the objects of their attention were birds perched among the grass.

They laughed in unison, and Haylee rolled her eyes in amusement. "Would you let them out while you're still up, please, so that they can go guard the yard?" Diane asked.

"Yeah. I wouldn't want to try and talk over their high-pitched yips." Getting them riled, she asked before opening the door, "You guys gonna go get them birds?" They bounced around as if to signify a response, flying out the door when it was finally opened.

The birds scattered into the air as the animals scrambled into the grass. Haylee had seen them do this countless times, but it never failed to still be funny.

Haylee took the seat across from her mother. The sunlight streaming in through the windows was already warming her back.

Smiling affectionately, her shopping list under her folded hands, Diane inquired, "What do you have going on today?"

Haylee grunted in irritation. Put simply, she responded, "Work."

"Hmm." Diane studied her, noting that she looked tired and worn down. She was tempted to scold her for working too much. But since she couldn't figure how to do it without sounding hypocritical, she only asked, "Work occupying a lot of your time lately?"

She nodded. "Probably too much," she acknowledged.

Her mother sighed before a frown took form on her face. Her doing, she supposed. Diane Jones had always worked more hours than the average person. But she had had to. No one was there to help, to share the load with, after her husband left. She made as much time for her daughter as she could and thought she had done as well as could be expected. What she hadn't wanted, hadn't anticipated, was passing on the excessive work ethic to Haylee.

She could tell that wasn't the only thing bothering her. Mothers knew. It was in the tone of voice over the phone, the subtle change of regular actions, and in the look in one's eyes. Haylee's enthusiasm was diminished, and she didn't go into details about her life. Something was wrong, and she had a good idea of what it was.

"Anything else on your mind?"

"I don't know….no, not really. Just a little stressed."

Diane pursed her lips in thought. The trick in getting a person to talk was to ease into the subject. "How is Scott?"

The flash of exasperation across Haylee's face told Diane she was on the right track. Haylee fiddled with her coffee mug to keep her hands busy. "Pretty good. Alright," she corrected.

"You can tell me honey."

Haylee blew out a long breath. It wasn't always easy to admit your problems, even to your own mother. "He's been driving me a little crazy actually."

"How so?"

"Well…." she trailed off. Did she really want to get into all the details? "He lost his job and I feel like he's being lazy. We got into a discussion and I found out his outlook on domestic matters don't quite match mine." She paused before deciding to confide in Diane. "Also, I fear that he hasn't been faithful."

The motherly instinct to protect had Diane cringing. "What makes you think that?"

"Let's just say I heard things."

Diane reached over to touch her daughter's arm. "No one deserves to be treated unfairly, and I know you, and I know you think that being unfaithful in a relationship is not fair. Is the source reliable, someone you trust?"

Haylee was alternating between biting her nails and biting her lip. "I used to think so, but I am not so sure now."

"What does your gut tell you?"

She didn't feel as though she couldn't answer. "I don't know."

Diane had sympathy for the situation. "Let me tell you what I think. You do know, one way or another. At times we block out our own intuition about things we don't *want* to be true. Figure it out for sure and decide what you want to do. Don't follow my example Haylee. I stayed with your father even though deep down I knew what he was up to. And it ended up hurting all the more when it was finally over. You don't want to end up like me, too jaded to try again."

Before her words could completely sink in, she continued, "Did Kathy's engagement cause you to really examine your own relationship?"

Haylee's head jerked toward her mother in shock. Confused, she asked, "What did you say?"

"Well, when the people close to us move forward, it can make us look at our paths…."

Before she could finish explaining, Haylee cut her off. "No, no. Kathy got engaged? And you heard before me? When did this happen?"

It was Diane's turn for confusion. "I'm sorry, I thought…I was sure you two would have talked." Because Kathy and her daughter were always very close, Diane treated Kathy as one of her own. And Kathy often addressed her as 'Mom'. It hadn't surprised her that she was one of Kathy's many calls the day before.

It had never occurred to her that Haylee would be in the dark, but then again, Kathy hadn't mentioned anything about Haylee either.

"She said it had happened Thursday night, but she didn't go into details."

Remembering her missed call and the subsequent text messages, Haylee recalled how she blew off Kathy's invitations. "She asked me to get together, but didn't say it was important. Now I feel like a jerk for brushing it aside. But how was I supposed to know if she didn't say?"

"All I can tell you is that you should always make time for the people important to you."

"Thanks, I think I feel worse now." Haylee rubbed her fingers against her temple. "I guess I have been too consumed in my problems to pay much attention to anyone else."

"You are a smart girl Haylee. It's probably about time you took care of your problems. More will always come your way, but I don't think anyone is entitled to let the same ones linger forever."

Chapter 16

～～～～～～～～～～

*H*aylee had a hard time staying calm during her open house. Her mother's words struck home, and yes, it was indeed time to sort out her problems. They surely wouldn't get solved on their own.

So far, she had spent the first hour alone. The weather was perfect for any outdoor activity and she supposed that families were outside together taking advantage of it. It frustrated her further that she was even there, seemingly for nothing.

But it wasn't a wasted Saturday. Her mom had given her a little push, and now she gave herself time to contemplate. As she sat in the empty house, with only the low sound of classical music to accompany her, she did her best to objectively view her situation. She could honestly say she had changed over the last several months, but to her dismay, in more negative ways than positive. She had always worked hard, but now she buried herself in her job. The motivation to do so may had been to avoid other issues she was facing. She knew there were more significant things in life than work, and wanted to maintain a balance. But here she was, working the umpteenth day in a row, on a day that most people spend on nothing but leisure.

Shaking out two aspirin from a bottle she carried in her purse with one hand, she rubbed her pulsing temple with the other, squeezing her eyes shut. She choked the pills down dry.

While her work wasn't constantly enjoyable, there was at least a concrete value that could be placed upon it. Her checks had been larger as of late hadn't they? An indulgent vacation could be a nice reward. The savings account she had was well over the projected amount she wanted.

Then, as if she had completely forgotten, she remembered why that account had been beefed up. As a cushion, to make sure all the bills were paid and so she could help Scott with his, too. Even though they hadn't combined finances, Haylee still felt obligated to see that Scott didn't sink because he was unemployed. When he moved in, she viewed them as a unit. And teams helped each other come through.

It could be easy to blame Scott for her workaholic tendencies, but she knew better than that. She thought it weak for people to blame others for the problems they created, for things they had done to themselves. Yet still, maybe he couldn't be to blame, but he could very well be a source of her troubles.

Haylee rose from her chair to peer out the bay window of the living room. A couple on bicycles rode past in the street, while two young boys across the street threw a baseball back and forth. A neighbor washed his car, while a woman who presumably was his wife tended the flowerbeds surrounding the front yard. All different people, but who had at least one thing in common. They had smiles on their faces. And that made Haylee envious.

The thin Timex on her wrist told her she had just fifteen

minutes to go before she could leave. The owners had politely asked her to 'lock up shop', after the open house was over. They were taking their two children camping for the night. Their youngest had talked candidly about the smores they would roast together. They were all so excited when she had arrived that Haylee might have been tempted to ask if she could join them in the simple fun. At least they trusted her to care for their house in their absence.

Normally, when she held an open house she hoped that as many people as possible would walk through the front door. Today she was happy only two had, and crossed her fingers that there wouldn't be any last-minute stragglers.

She dug her phone out of her purse that had been hidden in an empty kitchen cabinet. She switched it back on, shaking her head as she realized this was one of the rare occasions it was ever off. Scott had left her a message to say that he was going to have a poker night with some of the guys at Sam's house and wouldn't be home when she got there.

With her jaw set and teeth clenched, she let the phone drop to the counter with a bang. She had been thinking she would go home and have a serious conversation with Scott that evening, hopefully sort out some of the issues she was having with him. But now that plan was shot to hell, and wasn't it just like him to be unavailable when there was something important she wanted to speak with him about?

With a grunt of annoyance, she watched as a couple stood out front looking at a sheet they had pulled from the information box in the yard. She scolded herself for checking her messages before she left, or else she wouldn't have to force a smile if the couple walked in the door. She let out a sigh of relief when they chose to move past the house and be on their way.

Haylee gathered her things, changed into a tank top and jeans, and was in her car by five minutes past five. Fueled by her frustration, she took a small detour to drive past Sam's house in the hopes of having a few words with Scott face to face. Maybe she could even talk him into leaving with her.

It was easy to remember the way to Sam's; in fact, she would probably never forget it. After all, she did have a nasty encounter right outside of his house. Scott had been the hero that night. It was months ago, but as she neared the house, it began to feel like it all just happened yesterday.

Anxiety set in as she slowly drove past Sam's without seeing any cars in the driveway. By then, it was almost six o'clock and Scott's message had said they were all getting together at five.

"Hmm, okay….." she said out loud to herself. She had the phone in her hand as she pulled to the side of the curb, then thought better of it before dialing Scott's number. Her Mom had said something about listening to her gut, and right now it said not to call him. He didn't need a head's up that she knew he wasn't there.

The poker idea might have been nixed, so she still gave him the benefit of the doubt. She assumed they had instead opted to go to The Sport Cafe, their favorite bar. It had covered seating out front, and when it was warm, all the windows were put down to let the breeze in. A rail lined the inside of the windows so that you could sit watching people walking by. Some of Scott's friends specifically liked to watch the women that went shopping in the area.

She easily found a parking space on the street only a block away from the bar. She glided past the meter on the curb since no payment was required on the weekends, and slid her purse strap over her shoulder. On any given evening, the street she currently walked was loitered with people strolling from one establishment to another, who had long ago passed their threshold in alcohol tolerance. Therefore, she straightened her back, pushed on her sunglasses, and prepared to weave through the rowdy patrons.

Even though the sun was shining, the day's warmth was already beginning to give way to a cooler evening. Haylee folded her bare arms and wrapped them around her body to avoid a shiver when the wind blew. She walked past a few restaurants with their outdoor seating completely full, their seats alive with conversation and laughter. Shops had their doors propped open, not only to let fresh air in, but to encourage customers inside. Some people were feeling the chill too and were pulling on light jackets or sweaters, while others remained unaware to the slight temperature drop.

From across the street, Haylee slowed her pace as she neared the cafe's storefront. She caught a glimpse of someone who appeared to be Scott, but she didn't want to believe it was him. He was bellied up to the rail lining the street, next to a girl who was all over him. And he wasn't resisting. An unrestrained public display of affection, in the form of a kiss, followed. A few steps closer now, his identity was confirmed when she had a better angle of his face.

On the verge of tears, she turned away and began to head toward her car. But before she got very far, she felt the anger amid the hurt and opted to act on that emotion instead.

It took a lot to make Haylee very angry, to ball her fists at her side as they were at the moment. She put her practical self aside and this time refused to wait to face the situation until she was calmer. She did what anyone would probably advise against; she thought of every unconstructive situation and every unpleasant aspect of the relationship. The breaking point had been reached. She may have been walked on these past couple months and taken for granted.

But there came a time when a person just had to stand up for herself.

She was but a few steps from them. She remained on the street while they were tucked inside the tavern. Glass three feet high, with wood perched atop to serve as a ledge was the only thing that stood between them. Oblivious to their new company, Haylee shifted her weight all on her right foot, hands on her hips, and cleared her throat loudly to announce her arrival.

Scott visibly went from his golden tan shade to a pale white, as Haylee's wrath descended upon him. He wouldn't have thought she had it in her to challenge him amidst the situation, but that idea was fading as she stood facing him. He feared she might claw his eyes out, but Sarah was at his side unimpressed. He caught her rolling her eyes and folding her arms, but he nudged her hoping she would understand that meant to keep her mouth shut.

To further that thought, he leaned over and whispered to Sarah, "Why don't you run up to the bar and grab us some beers?"

Haylee butted in. "No, that won't be necessary Scott. She can stay for this."

Scott set his jaw. "Honey, can you keep your voice down? Everyone here doesn't need to know our business. We can leave and have a talk about this."

He only managed to set her off even more. "Oh don't honey me you asshole!" she blurted out in a volume anything but quiet. But her goal wasn't to make a spectacle of herself, so she did her best to lower her voice for her own sake.

She began with Sarah. "Look, I know that you don't know me, and I don't know you. Therefore, we hold no loyalties to each other and any 'rules' of friendship do not apply. So I will spare the name calling and refrain from placing all the blame on you. But really, I would think that as a woman, you would have higher standards for yourself as to how you treat and respect your own kind. But maybe it's just that you don't mind being the girl on the side. Perhaps you two deserve each other."

When Sarah began her retort, Haylee merely continued with a wave of her hand in Sarah's direction. "And you," she began as she swiveled toward Scott, "you do have some nerve don't you? To think I trusted you, and believed what you told me, when clearly I shouldn't have." She resisted the violent urge to slap him across the face, while also resisting the tears that threatened to form behind her eyes.

She hastily went on, preventing Scott from speaking. She didn't want to hear whatever he might have to say or be tempted to listen to an explanation. "My final thought, as juvenile as it may be, is that I think you are scum that isn't worthy of what I have to offer. Your things will be boxed up on my porch later this evening. Don't bother to knock on my door, even if I am at home, I won't be willing to talk to you."

It cut deep when Scott merely replied with a single word. "Okay," was all he said, and his body language lacked any show of remorse. In fact, it appeared as though he was undaunted by her behavior.

Haylee bit her lip, slowly shaking her head at him in disgust. She couldn't help but let one more utterance slip away before she left. "Fuck you," she sneered at him. With that, she stomped off toward her car, hearing Sarah snicker before she was out of earshot.

When she knew they could no longer see her, Haylee lifted her hand to wipe the few tears that had managed to trickle out. Blinking her eyes rapidly to clear her blurred vision, she wiped the evidence of her sorrow on her blue jeans. There would be plenty of time to cry in private, she thought. No use doing so in public in front of all these strangers.

A sudden panic washed over her. The routine she had become accustomed to was not only about to change, but was going to do a one hundred eighty-degree turn in the opposite direction. No more beer and pool with Scott on Friday nights, or Sunday matinees at the movies after her open houses. There wouldn't be anyone to cook dinner for or to bicker with over what to watch on television. She would wake alone in the morning for the first time in what felt like forever. And, although it was a blessing in disguise, she would have only herself to depend on and only herself to fend for.

"It's not like you didn't have that lifestyle before you idiot," she muttered under her breath.

Yet still, she couldn't clear the lump in her throat, or the hurt in her heart. She never had to mend a broken heart before but wished that it could be done overnight. A few beers, some chocolate chip cookie dough ice cream, and a twelve-hour sleep should be the healing remedy.

Haylee pulled down the sunglasses that had been perched atop her head to cover her red eyes. She cursed herself when she realized that in her daze, she had walked much farther then she needed to in order to reach her car.

Turning on her heel, she began in the path from which she had come. Part of her wanted to drown her sorrows in one of the bars she had passed along the way. Home, however, was the more viable option.

She contemplated the alienation her close friends had received as of late. Some with unreturned phone calls, some with repeated broken plans, and one who she flat-out snubbed because she had thought her a liar. Who would listen now as she sobbed her eyes out? She pondered that question as she continued, unable to come up with an answer.

As chance would have it, Haylee was about to turn the corner for the parking lot when she heard her name being called out. For a split second, she was hopeful that Scott was racing toward her to make amends, to say that she had misunderstood the entire situation somehow. But it registered that it wasn't Scott's voice she heard, as she looked over in the direction the shout came from. Familiar and male, but not Scott.

Pete's smiling face jogged across the street to catch up with her. She wanted to bolt, to run away quickly before he had a chance to converse with her. He would know something was wrong immediately, no matter what excuses she concocted. And even though she was just wondering who she could talk to about this, she wasn't ready right now.

Pete leapt up on the curb, obviously in a good mood. The crowd of people he had parted with paused to wait for him, but he waved them on.

"Hey! Its good to see you, how've you been?" He asked her.

Haylee deliberately broadened her grin. "Good," she claimed. "How about you?"

"Ugh, busy. I'm getting acclimated to the new job, new house, and new surroundings."

After their last time together, Pete longed to see Haylee again. He had feared it might be awkward, or worse yet, that she wouldn't want to hang around him because of their chemistry. He had intended to contact her prior to running into her, but time had slipped away from him.

"Aside from that, everything is first-rate."

"Great. I suppose you are getting all settled in then?"

She was about to start her fabricated explanation of why she had to be going, but he asked, "What brings you this way? Can I steal an hour from you and buy you a beer? There's a group of us meeting up down the street."

She hesitated, knowing she would feel guilty if she said no. She had all but ignored him since she had last been to his house. A group atmosphere was safe ground and she wanted them to be friends. Although, she rapidly became aware that she no longer had to worry about the dynamics of their relationship. There was no longer anyone else in the picture.

"I don't know...," she trailed off. To say the least, she wasn't in the mood to be around other people. Particularly, happy people that were having fun. She wanted to wallow in her grief and let herself be upset.

It was then Pete's radar took effect. "What's wrong? Did you have a rough day?"

Haylee sighed, looked down to her feet. "You could say that. Pretty rotten actually. I probably wouldn't be the best company."

Pete persisted. "Did you have other plans?"

"No," Haylee admitted.

"Well then, you can't go home and be alone. It always helps to spill the beans to another person, and then you'll feel better. We're a lively bunch, we'll make you forget your lousy day."

She doubted it. But next thing she knew, she was being pulled by the hand in the direction Pete's friends had taken.

It occurred to her that they might be headed to Sports, where Scott was most likely still holed up. Frantically, she stopped in her tracks.

Pete spun around, startled by her sudden, flustered halt. She tried to blow it off as best she could and act casual. "Um, where are we going?"

Pete raised an eyebrow, astonished this was the ever-important question she so abruptly stopped their forward movement for. Slowly he answered, "The...Tavern...?" as though that may or may not be the right response.

Haylee shrugged and jammed her hands in her pockets. "Oh, okay. Just curious."

She wasn't just curious, but Pete didn't probe. Haylee was glancing through a shop window, most likely to avert his gaze. Pete supposed she was aware of his perceptive nature. He was by no means a mind reader; he merely saw the body language and facial expressions that most failed to recognize. If she didn't want to share her problems, then he would be sure to drop the subject.

It would not be an easy feat, however, seeing as though he felt compelled to help her. She fascinated him by just being who she was, and the thought that she was troubled disturbed him. A face like hers should never wear a frown.

As they neared their destination, Pete's words went through one of Haylee's ears and out the other. She kept discreetly peeking in the direction of Sports, fearful Scott would round the corner. She knew that if she saw him again so soon, the hurt would be immense, especially with Sarah on his arm. Haylee gave a cursory 'yeah' or 'um-hum' intermittently to keep Pete talking and keep the focus off her.

Pete pulled out a chair for her at a table with an array of people. He made introductions, but Haylee could not recall a single name, though they all seemed genuinely pleased to have her join them. Thankfully, no one began to ask questions, they all went back to their own conversations after welcoming her. Maybe she could handle it after all.

She began to relax after her first beer had been consumed. In good company, Scott left Haylee's mind, if only for the time being.

She chatted with one of Pete's coworkers, whose name

was Evan. Evan, like herself, had grown up in the area so they at least had that in common. Evan spoke of the areas of the city he would like to purchase a home in, and asked Haylee's opinion.

"I think those are great neighborhoods," she told him. She hesitated for a moment before asking, "Did I already tell you what I did for a living?"

Evan shook his head, laughing. "No. But you are the same Haylee that helped Pete right? I assumed there couldn't be two."

"No, I suppose there wouldn't be. Yes, I helped him out, but he made it real easy."

Evan tauntingly exposed his friend. "Well, the way he went on about you, I would have thought you were realtor of the year."

A knee-jerk reaction, Haylee blushed. "No, not quite." Then she continued, "at least not yet."

Evan glanced over at Pete who had begun to eye the two of them. He gave Pete a sly smile, and decided to take it upon himself to put in a good word for his new friend who had clearly become smitten with the girl in front of him.

"You know, I haven't known Pete long, but from what I can tell, he really is a standout guy."

Haylee marveled at the abrupt change of topic. "Yeah, I gathered as much too."

Pete dragged his hand across his neck, gesturing to Evan to put the axe on the discussion. Ignoring Pete, Evan went on, unaware of the fact that but only hours ago she had been taken. "I think he has a boyish little crush on you."

Oblivious, Haylee's brow furrowed. "What do you mean? We're just friends, no big deal." She had chalked this one up as she always had, presuming it was purely a physical attraction.

"Oh, I think if Pete had it his way, that wouldn't be so…" Evan trailed off when Haylee stood.

"Hold that thought Evan. I have to go to the ladies' room."

After she scurried off, Pete parked himself in her chair in her absence. "What are we, teenagers here?" he asked Evan. "I don't need you to present a girl with my 'will you go out with me note'." Evan shrugged innocently. "Besides, she's with someone."

"Hmmph. Too bad," Evan told him. "She seems pretty cool."

"Agreed. Where did she run off to? She's kind of jumpy today."

"Apparently, nature was calling. She didn't even let me finish my sentence, which was odd. I thought maybe I pissed her off somehow."

"Hmmm," was all Pete said.

"Then again, she could have trouble controlling her bladder, or something of the sort," Evan joked as he punched Pete playfully in the arm. "I wouldn't bring that up though," he warned.

Chapter 17

$\mathscr{B}$efore she rounded the corner to the restrooms, Haylee looked over her shoulder to observe. She could still see Scott and Sarah through the front windows. Instinct had her jumping out of her chair in case they decided to visit this particular establishment. She wanted to avoid any further confrontations, and she figured she could find a way to slink out if needed. Scott was rather unpredictable when intoxicated, as he most likely was by now, and Haylee knew if he saw her with Pete and Evan he would make a scene.

Haylee practically gagged as she watched the two of them, a reflex that helped to keep the anguish at bay. She crossed her fingers that they would continue walking.

Her concern was realized when Scott entered through the front door. Sarah, however, was not trailing behind. She scanned the sidewalk and caught Sarah with her cell phone glued to her ear, crossing the street. At least now she only had one pair of eyes to elude. She would have to make a hasty exit in case Sarah was coming back.

She needed to take a moment first to think of what she

would tell Pete and the others. She pushed the heavy oak door to the women's room open, and turned on the faucet from one of the three sinks lined up against an eight-foot mirror. Splashing the cold water on her face felt amazingly refreshing. She pulled her compact out of her purse after toweling off her cheeks, and gave her nose a light dusting. She was relieved that her eyes weren't as red and puffy as she had predicted.

Haylee thought it best if she quietly exited the building, and then called from her car with some lame excuse that she would devise on the way. It was good that Pete had offered to buy her a drink because she didn't want to take the time to get her bill and pay.

Scott was bellied up to the mahogany bar lining the wall, his back turned to her. She could see through a framed, mirrored beer advertisement that he was looking down, punching keys on his phone. The crowd was thick and she was confident she could sneak out without being seen. She made her way past the first few tables between her and the door, and coyly slid past a group that blocked Pete's view of her. The room inside was suddenly suffocating, and Haylee wanted nothing more to step out on the sidewalk with the last few dimming beams of sunlight raining down on her.

A server with tray full of cocktails stopped Haylee in her tracks. The girl was concentrating so hard on not sloshing the drinks out of the glasses that she persisted on her path without even a glance in Haylee's direction. Not wanting to be the asshole to bump her arm and send the liquid flying and the glassware crashing to the floor, Haylee waited for her to pass by, impatiently.

That pause gave Evan just enough time to catch up to her. "Hey, where are you off to? You weren't deserting us were you?" He gave her a friendly tug, flinging his arm on top of her shoulder. "Look, I wasn't trying to upset you or anything."

Haylee felt foolish, and reassured him. "No, you didn't upset me, I just….was…." she tapered off.

As she searched her brain for a reasonable explanation, Pete joined them. "Hey! We were talking about starting a game of pool." He handed her the stick he held in his hands. "Will you be my partner?"

Haylee glowered over Pete's shoulder at the tables in the distance, lined in a row. They were all only but a few feet from the bar, and all in plain view for Scott.

She pushed the offered pool stick back toward Pete. "Actually, I have to be going."

The reply on Scott's phone from Sam said 'walking into The Tavern in one minute'. Scott swiveled in his chair to face the entry so he could signal him over. The ever increasing noise in the place made it impossible to call out Sam's name and be heard. Sam was going to keep him company for the remainder of the evening until he felt like meeting up with Sarah again later on.

As he surveyed the crowd now in front of him, he searched for familiar faces out of habit. The tables were filling up fast with people and pitchers of pilsners. He observed as one brave guy interrupted a group of women engrossed in their own conversation and laughed to himself when he saw the girls rolling their eyes and folding their arms. Undeterred and oblivious, he carried on fueled by liquid courage. Scott wondered how long it would take him to get the hint.

He shifted his gaze slightly to the right, just as a man with his back to him bent over to retrieve a pool stick that was falling to the floor. Had he not moved, Scott may not have caught a glimpse of Haylee otherwise. But now he watched her, one male arm slung around her and another engaging her from the front.

What a fucking hypocrite! was all Scott could think. An hour ago, she was yelling at him for being with Sarah, and now here she was the center of attention of two different men. How dare she act all innocent and hurt when she had been doing the exact same thing he had all along?

Scott thought she could use a taste of her own medicine and sauntered his way over to where she was standing. She'll see what public humiliation is all about.

He hadn't expected the pool stick to come right back to him, so he was bent over plucking it off the floor. Evan began arguing with Haylee over why she should stay put, while she insisted that she had to go. Pete couldn't fathom what had happened to have made her act so strangely.

Turns out he would get an answer very soon. Pete could feel someone behind him, and turned to look after seeing Haylee's face go white.

"Can I help you?" Pete asked. He had no idea this was Scott, let alone the knowledge of the day's events between the former couple.

Scott ignored the question, choosing instead to immediately barrel into Haylee.

"Quite the little tramp aren't you?" Even Scott may have admitted that was harsh, and in sober times, characteristically untrue of her. But he was too busy being angry to think of being the least bit kind. She wasn't going to speak to him the way she did then behave in this fashion.

Haylee's full lips parted open, then, slowly her jaw fell until her mouth was fully agape. Scott added, "I see that you wasted no time finding someone else, although I bet this was going on all along. How dare you give me hell when you are doing the exact same thing?"

Haylee tried to defend herself. "Scott, you've got it all wrong, but I don't want to discuss it here. Maybe we should step outside." For the life of her, Haylee couldn't understand why Scott's opinion of her mattered at this point.

Scott's temper continued to flare the more he thought about the situation. His impression of Haylee was changing drastically, the way it can only when you feel completely wronged by another person.

"Tell you what. It doesn't matter. You were never worth my time anyway."

It was Haylee's turn to feel her temper rise. *I wasn't worth his time?* Tears of anger swelled into her eyes, and she felt a breakdown about to occur.

Pete, standing on the sidelines, quietly dumbfounded up until this point, felt compelled to step in to mediate. It wasn't his problem or any of his business, but Haylee looked as though she might crumble if she didn't get out of the confrontation. Plus, it was extremely hard for him to listen as Scott spoke to her in this manner.

Pete lightly placed his left hand on Scott's shoulder to get his raging focus off Haylee. For all he knew, Scott could turn violent any second. At least, he wouldn't doubt it by the look of him.

"Hey man, why don't you let me buy you a drink and we can cool off for a minute."

Scott threw Pete's hand off his shoulder in one shift motion. "Butt out. This doesn't concern you."

Pete put his arm back down by his side, convinced Scott was unmanageable at the moment. He took a step forward, with the intention of going to Haylee to persuade her to walk away until Scott had a chance to calm down.

Scott misread Pete's movement as a threatening gesture, thinking he was going to get in his face. Proactively, he gave Pete one hard shove with both hands, sending Pete flying into Evan. Evan caught Pete, preventing him from stumbling to the ground, and helped Pete get his balance.

Scott advanced slowly enough to give Haylee the opportunity to get between him and the other two. She balled her hands into fists against Scott's chest and planted her feet as best she could to keep him from moving.

"Let it be," she pleaded. "Yell and scream at me, I'm who you're mad at. Leave them alone."

Scott grabbed Haylee's wrists tight. "I would. But right now, he's royally pissed me off."

He threw her arms down, tried to step around her, but she persisted. She tugged and pulled, succeeded in staying in his way.

Completely irritated with her reluctance to back off, Scott forcefully pushed his arm into Haylee's body, which ended up swiping her across the neck. Stunned, she fell back while gasping for the breath that had been knocked out of her. Small dark spots appeared in her vision from the direct hit.

Haylee sat on the dirty floor, sticky where drinks had been spilled, and gathered herself best she could. She watched the rest of the quarrel unfold from below.

In the instant Pete witnessed Haylee's fall at Scott's hand, he no longer desired to try the peaceful, verbal route. If this was the way the asshole wanted it, then by all means, he would have it.

He hadn't been in a fight since grade school. That's *if* you could call a tackle and roll in the dirt a fight. But he planned on being defensive. When, and surely if, Scott swung at him, he would duck, but at least he would be certain who started it. Merely defending himself, Haylee would have to help him feel less immature about this later. But the fact that Scott had the audacity to assault a woman would help him feel better as well.

Scott let one punch fly through the air, but missed completely with only so much as a sidestep from Pete. He tripped on his own toes from the force he put into it, off balance from the alcohol. Scott, on the other hand, had been in his share of fights, so he knew not to lift his head immediately and risk a blow to the face. Instead, he charged into Pete, throwing him and himself onto a table. The contents clattered down to where there feet had just been.

Haylee felt relieved when two employees came over to interfere before anything worse could happen. They pulled Scott back on his feet, putting distance between the feuding men. Pete sat up on the table, relieved as well that he wasn't going to be leaving with some hideous wounds or bruises.

The Tavern's employees didn't waste any time escorting Scott to the door. A simple 'we don't want to see you in here the rest of the night' was all he received in parting, as he was thrust outside. One of them waited to be sure he wouldn't try to enter again, and the other made his way over to where Haylee stood, hands cupped over her face, apologizing profusely to Pete.

"Look," he told them. "I saw most of what happened before I could get over here. Normally, we would kick out everyone involved. But it was obvious that that guy was the instigator, and you were trying to hold his crazy ass off. Actually, I would recommend you stay put for awhile, in case he's planning on waiting for you outside. Give him a chance to cool off. If need be, we can call you a cab to meet you out front."

Pete stood, smoothed out his rumpled clothing. "Thanks. Might take you up on that cab shortly."

The worker nodded, and made his way back to his duties. A bartender had already come over with a broom, sweeping up some broken class, compliments of Scott. Most of the patrons had gone back to their own business, essentially forgetting the spectacle. A few still looked on and whispered, and Haylee wished she didn't feel like she was on display.

Pete said, "Hey Ev, do you mind telling our friends everything is okay before they all come up asking questions? I can see some of them trying to make their way over here through the crowd of people. They probably couldn't see what happened."

"Sure, no prob."

After Evan left, Haylee apologized once more. Pete told her, "Don't worry about it. It wasn't your fault. I can't stand to see a man put his hands on a woman, so I was ready to wallop him. But I would appreciate some insight as to why he was so upset. What happened?"

Haylee pulled out a chair to the abandoned table next to them. Somewhat reluctantly, she gave Pete the condensed, although painfully honest, version of what had transpired that day, and even included the back story behind it.

Pete shook his head in sympathy, and laid his hand over Haylee's folded ones perched on the table. "That's terrible. I know it hurts, but you'll get through it. You deserve much better than him anyhow."

Haylee mustered a hint of a smile. In the short time since everything had happened, it had suddenly become so clear just how unsuitable Scott was for her, and how befuddled she had been. She had put so much into it, to make it work, and had blindsided herself of Scott's true self. But now, that spell had been broken.

"Actually, he has made it really easy to start getting over it all. Sure, I won't be able to turn love off like a switch and I'll miss what was good for awhile, but I was completely ignorant of what the situation was truly like. All I'll have to do is picture the debacle here, or remind myself of his infidelities, and I'm pretty sure that will help the hurt to subside significantly. I think our relationship had been ending for awhile now."

Pete nodded. "I'm glad you see it that way. I have to admit I'm not impressed with him, so maybe it's all for the best. You'll have to let me know if you need anything."

She took a moment to appreciate Pete's kindness toward her, knowing full well that kindness had been lacking from Scott. It was a welcome change. "I will." She also understood that the scope of his kindness was not limited to a friendship. "It might take awhile to need anything though."

She smiled then and leaned over to kiss his cheek. He escorted her out and followed her to her mother's house after they both decided they had had enough action for one night. Just in case, Haylee had opted to stay at Diane's house. She didn't believe Scott would give her any trouble, but Pete had insisted that she didn't stay at her place until she had changed the locks.

Once inside, she watched from the living room window as Pete pulled away. She sighed, feeling lucky to have people who cared about her. In no way did she want to take advantage of him, but she was confident Pete could help her learn to trust again and make her want to try again. That would have to wait for the time being, but, perhaps, eventually.

Her Mom was waiting in the kitchen ready to help mend her daughter, strawberries, chocolate, and champagne in tow.

Looking around, Haylee couldn't help but ask, "What's all this?"

Diane handed her a flute filled to the brim. "We're celebrating."

Haylee merely cocked one eyebrow, wondering how they could possibly celebrate in the midst of all the tribulations.

She had wanted to put a positive spin on the situation,

not only to cheer Haylee up, but to encourage her to charge forward. When Haylee just stared not saying anything, Diane lifted her flute in a toast. "To new beginnings. When one door closes, another opens." She thought about it for a second then added, "hopefully more than one, and a few windows too."

They tapped glasses before taking sips.

Chapter 18

It took Haylee several weeks, but she got her life back to normal, as it was prior to Scott. She hadn't wasted any time ridding her home of Scott's belongings and anything that reminded her of him. Surprisingly, Scott was cordial when he came to pluck his things off her front porch, asking only cursory questions like, 'had she remembered to pack his CDs that had been intermingled with hers'. And once again, he was detached and nonchalant, making no attempt to apologize or plead for her to take him back.

It stung that he could brush her off so easily, like a pesky ant at a picnic. He had cut her and she bled from it, but she was certain she would heal the wound and only have a tiny scar left to remind her of what she had gone through, what she had learned from everything. After he had left her house, she hadn't heard from him, nor did she make any attempt to contact him.

There had been an immediate, though mild, depression at first, mostly out of humiliation and shame for herself. It had drained her emotionally, and for the first day, physically as well. She had thought it possible that someone had beaten her while she had slept at Diane's, but that wasn't the case. She decided that if she felt the need, she would let herself mope around in misery, albeit temporarily, but the tears she had shed in her mother's company that first weekend were apparently all she had needed.

She suspected there was a sense of relief she had, now that Scott was gone, that alleviated the sadness. She hadn't felt like herself while with him, and it was a lesson she had learned to never let another so fully alter her identity. The change in lifestyle wasn't the issue, but the change in her attitude and personality was.

A sincere apology had been due to Wendy, and so she gave it. Wendy had been standoffish at first, having felt distrusted and discarded, but relented after hearing all of what Haylee had to say. Haylee did not bother to defend herself, but rather credited herself with all the blame. She promised if Wendy only forgave her for such a poor show of friendship, that it would never happen again. To further the peace, she begged Wendy to come to dinner with her, Haylee's treat, so they could catch up with each other. By the end of that evening, it felt normal between the two of them again.

Kathy received her share of apologies as well, but gave her longtime friend an earful before accepting.

"It really pissed me off how unavailable you were for anyone but him. You weren't even available when I wanted to tell you about getting engaged." Kathy sounded off. "It's got to be a balance you know."

Racked with guilt, her head was already bowed. "I know. I feel really bad I wasn't there for you, and I'm sorry."

"You can't treat everyone else who cares about you like dirt. Or well, you shouldn't want to."

"I don't want to."

Kathy pursed her lips. "I suppose you could make it up to me with a fabulous engagement party," she teased. "Complements of my best friend."

Haylee had already contemplated the idea, but hesitated to bring it up first because she didn't want her friends to think she was trying to buy their forgiveness. "That I could possibly do," Haylee admitted. "But, we'll have to keep it somewhat low key. I'm not rich you know," she mocked.

"Too bad for you." Kathy then added, "Too bad for me, too. I would totally mooch off you if you were." With that, she gave Haylee a friendly nudge on the shoulder. "Seriously though, Scott was an asshole, or at least I thought so. I didn't want to say anything because, at least at first, you seemed to be happy. And you had never really given anyone a chance before so I didn't want to come between that."

Haylee looked out to the retention pond in the distance behind Kathy's apartment. The last streams of sun reflected off the water giving the ripples a subtle shimmer. Three ducklings were gliding across the water, following their mother. Haylee snickered to herself, noting no male accompanied them. Maybe all members of the animal kingdom had a bitch of a time with that gender too.

In response to Kathy she said, "I understand that. I may have alienated you even more had you said what you wanted to say. I admire that discretion. But I have to say, next time you have full permission to state your opinions of character. I don't plan on repeating these mistakes."

Kathy leaned back on the bench the two of them sat on and crossed one leg over the other. "Good to hear. You can count on me to open my mouth if you really want me to." To emphasize, "IF you really me want to. I've heard I can be brash."

Haylee snorted. "Hmm, maybe just a tad," she said

sarcastically. "That's why I'm impressed you didn't chew me out earlier."

"Well, none of my business I guess. May be the first time I actually thought of it that way. But I have to ask, why did you stay with him so long after you started to see it going downhill? You made it sound as though you were miserable with him at the end there."

Haylee absently toyed with a stone that was between her feet before brushing the hair out of her eyes. "I was," she confessed. "But a big part of me felt like it was my fault that things weren't working out between us, and I was compelled to do everything I could to make it right."

"Well it takes two. It wouldn't have been all your fault. Were you afraid to feel walked out on again?" Kathy had a good understanding of the way Haylee felt about her father, and how she viewed his absence over the years.

It was hard to admit. Not because she was talking to Kathy, but because she had thought she made peace with all of those feelings long ago.

"Yes. I was reluctant to give anyone the chance to even do so. But then when I did give Scott a chance, I thought it would be my fault if I couldn't hang on to him. That I wasn't good enough if he left. So I wanted to do everything I could to not let that happen. I thought we could get through problems and make it work."

She paused. "It would have helped if I had had a willing partner to begin with. He made it clear that I was never that important to him. His toy, at best."

Kathy gave her friend a pat on the back, pulled her in to hug her. "You weren't his toy. But you are right that he didn't value or appreciate what you had to offer. Instead, he took advantage of your weakness. Next time, you'll have to choose someone who complements your imperfections."

Haylee nodded, but was frowning at herself.

Kathy continued, "You won't end up alone as long as you are willing to try again. Most people don't find the right person on their first try. It takes work figuring out what you really want out of another person and what they want out of you."

"I think you've said that last part before."

"I have. This time, I think you are actually listening instead of assuming I am feeding you some bullshit on why you should give some guy another chance."

A smile ran across Haylee's face. "You *are* full of bullshit though, aren't you?"

Kathy's face puckered in offense. "I see. I at least made you feel better enough so that you could insult me." She flipped up her middle finger. "Is that all it takes?"

Haylee's expression sobered. "You know I was kidding. You did make me feel better though. However, I'll need plenty more consoling in the near future so please have more ready."

Kathy turned toward Haylee. "I can do that. Now, or more later?"

Haylee considered. "More later. Let's go inside and get a notebook so I can write down a guest list. We have an engagement party to plan."

Her hand was lifted so they could both admire her round-cut solitaire diamond as light danced off its surface when she fluttered her fingers. Kathy added, "And a wedding. I'll need ample help from my maid of honor. That is, if you accept."

Relief washed over Haylee with the realization that things between the two of them were getting back to normal. "I'd be honored," Haylee declared.

Ample help had not been an understatement. Half of

Haylee's free time was devoted to something wedding related as of late. The engagement party she had given had been a great success even though she kept it small. Kathy had been happy to have an excuse to get some friends together to celebrate. In the past few weeks, Haylee had been pulled along to numerous reception venues, had attended bridal shows, oohed and aahed over numerous white gowns, and had sifted through bridal magazines right alongside Kathy.

She sighed to herself, thinking how everything was coming together nicely, and quickly. Kathy had chosen October of that year for their wedding, since she was set on fall nuptials. Otherwise, 'she would have to wait a whole year and a half' as she had put it, and the impatient girl had deemed that an unfeasible courting period. That gave her five short months to set everything in place. And Haylee shared in feeling that time crunch. But she had to admit, it was fun.

Luckily, Kathy had not run into any major obstacles as of yet. Planning timelines she had plucked off the Internet instructed her to have half the wedding planned six months ago, warning that venues and vendors could be booked a year or more in advance. It was true that some she had looked into had been unavailable, but she had been more than pleased with the options that had been left. She had reserved a beautiful church and reception site, two of the things she had worried about most. It wasn't an easy feat in such short notice, but she had pulled it off.

Now, Haylee was pulling in to CBT's, the caterer that Kathy had finally chosen. She carried with her a lofty check made out as a deposit for their services, and a finalized menu for the reception that Haylee was quite impressed with. Guests had a choice of filet mignon which they could have oscar style with crab, hollandaise, and asparagus. Or salmon with a berre blanc sauce with wild mushroom risotto. There was a vegetarian option as well, though Haylee didn't think there were any vegetarians attending, and the meal included salads, breads, and different side dishes. The dinner was to be served since the bride did not particularly care for buffet-style, citing as the reason she wanted everyone to be able to sit and relax. Haylee honestly thought Kathy was scared she would trip and fall with a plate of food in her hand. But she kept that to herself.

"Doesn't this sound really good?" she asked and passed the menu over.

Pete took the menu and scanned it over. "Yeah it does, do we get a sampling since we are dropping the money off?"

Haylee snickered. "I wish. We missed the sampling part. Kathy and Jake did that a few weeks ago. It was only for the bride and groom, or else I'm sure we would have all packed around the table."

Pete had voluntarily joined her in wedding errands more than she could have possibly asked him to. In the weeks following Scott's tirade and the subsequent breakup, Pete had provided a friendly ear and a shoulder to lean on. He had been there for her, but never pushed or made advances on her. On the contrary, it was she who had jumped over the wall of friendship to a different realm when she had felt she was ready. Since that time, what they had together had progressed slowly but surely into a deep, meaningful relationship. They were crazy about one another, even if Haylee was a little reluctant to admit how devoted she was. Despite initiating the romance, her guard was up, and she wasn't vocal about her feelings.

"And remind me why this couldn't be mailed in? It's a little out of the way for you."

Haylee glanced over at Pete's smiling face and answered, "Because Kathy thought it would be a good idea to wait until the last minute to choose this caterer, and they told her this would be the last day they would hold her date without payment. Had to get them their money today or they were going to call other people that had requested the same day who would pay them immediately."

Surprised at the answer, Pete commented, "I think it's very amusing and contradictory that Kathy is so impatient herself but procrastinates excessively. Doesn't she realize that many people are like her and hate to wait?"

"I guess it's one of those things that's okay for her to do but not anyone else. I think she actually said that to me once," she paused. "We all have our flaws, right?"

His grin widened. "I don't know. I can't find a single one with you." He brought her hand up to his lips to kiss it.

"Yeah, right." She appreciated the sweet gesture, but nonetheless pulled her arm back down to her side. "You haven't looked very hard then. Get real."

He pushed the front door to the store open, held it out for her. "I was being serious."

The smirk on her face subsided almost as quickly as it came. Her breath caught in her throat, and she felt a pressing need to immediately turn around on her heels and run out the door. She was left speechless as she could only stare into the face on the other side of the counter. Her father stood, staring right back.

She recognized him easily because he hadn't seemed to age a bit. The face, the eyes, all the same as she had last remembered seeing them years ago. He wore a pressed white button-down shirt with a sharp blue tie, black-rimmed glasses, and a name tag she couldn't quite read. But she didn't have to. She knew it would say 'Ken Jones'.

She looked up to Pete with wide eyes and asked him if he would mind waiting for her in the car. Pete knew the basics of her life history, but she didn't want to have to deal with the awkwardness the situation would give rise to. After all, she had no idea what would come out of her Dad's mouth.

Pete furrowed his brow, obviously perplexed as to what was going on, but obliged by slipping back out the door. When it closed behind him, Haylee hesitantly walked up to the counter.

After a moment of searching for words, Ken broke the silence. "Hello Haylee. How are you?" Certainly a trivial question coming from his mouth, but it was all that initially came to mind. His thoughts went blank when he recognized what a beautiful young woman she had grown to be, even though he had had time to prepare what he would say to her. A client named Kathy had called to inform him that Haylee Jones would be dropping off the deposit check for her.

Haylee didn't know which route to take, how to act. On one hand, this was a rare opportunity for her to let him know exactly what she thought of him and his past actions, and on the other, she was still a daughter that loved her father regardless. She chose a guarded middle ground.

"Quite well actually. You?"

He turned down the ringer on the phone so it would be easier to ignore if it rang. "I'm good. I understand you are dropping off a deposit for your friend?"

"Um yeah." Fine. So he was going to be cold and keep this to business. She would have to take her time so she could have a minute to think of the things she would like to get off her chest while she was here. "Its right here," she said as she dug the check out of the purse.

She half flung it over to him, dropping the menu down as well. "These are their final choices, food-wise."

"I see." He picked up the paper, pretended to read the contents. He had practically memorized what this bride wanted he had talked to her so many times. As the owner, he liked to frequently consult with the costumers. He was merely stalling so he could work up the guts to beg her forgiveness. The fear wasn't for the act itself, but that the apology wouldn't be the least bit accepted.

Haylee cleared her throat. "Alright, well, you can call Kathy if you have any questions. I have to be going." She was losing the courage to voice her feelings. She turned to walk back out to the fresh air outside, back to where she could breathe again.

She only got two steps, already contemplating the decision she was making, when Ken spoke up again.

"Please wait."

Haylee's heart tightened in her chest as she slowly turned on her heel. She raised her eyebrow and asked, "What?"

"Do you have a minute I could speak with you?"

Trying to match the coldness she felt from him, she told him, "I suppose."

Ken gestured to a small table to her right, walked up to pull out the chair for her. She sat, and waited.

He almost reached out for her hand, but placed them folded on the table instead. He let out a long breath and began.

"I know an apology alone won't cut it, but I am sorry I haven't been in contact with you. Believe it or not, I have wanted to for some time, but for one reason or another I didn't."

Haylee clenched her teeth, willed the tears to stop forming. "And those reasons would be?"

"At first I thought you would be better off with only your mother, as I hardly thought I was doing well as your father. The weekends you would have been in my care, I was too busy spending time out with friends or women. Selfish, I know. All I can say is that it was a bad time in my life, and

I'll spare you those details. I'm sure they'll sound like mere excuses anyhow."

Haylee was silent as she let him continue.

"Then later on I had the notion that you wouldn't want anything to do with me since I had spent so much time neglecting you. I figured you despised me for leaving you and your mother, and I wouldn't blame you. But I knew when you walked in here it was my chance to tell you I was sorry for never being there, and I regret it immensely."

There was no stopping a few tears from falling. In truth, Haylee had waited years to hear him say just that.

"It hurt. I missed you so much. It made me feel like I had done something wrong and that you were punishing me."

Now he did reach for her hand on top of the table, and was comforted when she didn't yank it away. "No. It was and always will be my fault. I hope that gradually, over time, you will let me be part of your life. And maybe I can try to make up for some of the time I lost."

She thought she would be angry and want to yell at him for what he did, or didn't do for that matter. But strangely, she felt satisfied with his apology, with the knowledge of his regret. And pleased that he cared enough to want to make an attempt at making it up to her. She believed forgiveness could mend her heart, if she chose to give it. Hadn't she been provided plenty of clemency in the last few weeks? It was her turn to give some, even if it wasn't going to be easy.

"It'll take some time, but I would like that. With one condition. Let's not spend time discussing what did or didn't happen in the past. We've both had plenty of time to think about it and deal with it in our own way, so let's focus on moving forward from here. It was enough for me to know you are sorry."

Ken squeezed her hand tighter, impressed by his daughter's ability to forgive. "Deal."

Pete braced himself as Haylee walked back to the car and got in the passenger's seat. From the looks of her red cheeks and teary eyes, he was prepared to hear bad news, but surprisingly, she smiled after she sat down.

"Sorry that took so long, but thanks for waiting," she told him.

"Sure. Want to fill me in? Or do you not want to talk about it?"

She did fill him in. About the apology, about the future she and Ken discussed after she told him she would let him in her life. She explained the weight that had been lifted off her shoulders knowing she had never done anything wrong to provoke her dad's departure. The clouds that had hung over her head had finally parted to let the sunlight through, sunlight that she needed to begin a long, overdue healing process. And with Pete, and her dad back in her life, she believed it could begin.

Chapter 19

$\mathcal{T}$he months leading up to Kathy's wedding flew by. That was the thought that ran through Haylee's head as she walked down the aisle of Saint Luke's church ahead of Kathy. Everything was in place, and now was the time to just simply enjoy. They had faced a bit of drama over Kathy's hairdresser being late, and being the jittery bride, Kathy had panicked thinking she wouldn't have anyone to style her hair or her bridesmaids'. The whole timetable would be thrown off and they would be late. But it was resolved an hour later after the woman showed up with another co-worker in tow to compensate for being late.

She did her duties. She held Kathy's bouquet of red roses while the couple said their vows, and she fixed the long beaded train of Kathy's dress after she took her place at the altar. She wished she could see Kathy's face instead of the back of her head—a downside to being in the wedding party—but she could imagine the love and elation her friend was conveying. She had demonstrated nothing but while they sat waiting for the music to start. The ceremony was short, but sweet, and Haylee watched as the front rows of family blotted at their eyes.

At one point, she caught sight of Pete in his seat and he was watching her intently. He seemed to jump when she made eye contact as though he wanted to observe her undetected. Something strange was on his face, she thought it might be anxiety, but maybe he was just bored to be there. She found that most men didn't enjoy weddings nearly as much as she did.

After the pictures were taken at the church, they rode to a nearby hotel for the reception. Haylee once again surveyed the crowd in her seat at the head table looking for Pete. She hoped he wasn't irritated to have to spend half the night sitting alone at a wedding for a couple he barely knew yet. In her defense, she had warned him that she would be tied up until after dinner was over, and he had still agreed to come. But there he was seated, pushing around the food on the plate in front of him, looking distant.

Her mind was already wrapping itself around ways she could make this up to him, to show her appreciation. And she said as much to him when they finally had a moment alone to speak.

"Hang in there, the torture is almost over," she jokingly told him. She had taken the empty chair next to him at his table, which had been deserted by everyone else that had sat there.

He managed what resembled a smile as he reached for her hand, but couldn't hide the tremor in his grip. He could tell she noticed it too.

"I don't think this is torture. True, it would have been more fun to converse with you over dinner then these complete strangers, but I'm not complaining. They were all entertaining people." He cleared his throat as the music turned to a slower note. "Now why don't I be the picture-perfect date here, and voluntarily twirl you around the dance floor." He paused before adding, "To the envy of the other women I can already see tugging their reluctant men by the hand."

She let him pull her up out of the chair. "I wouldn't mind," she admitted.

As Lionel sang of endless love, Haylee threw her arms around Pete's neck and, looking up into his eyes, was still fretting over his expression.

"Are you okay? What's the matter?"

"Nothing. Promise," he added when she kept staring at him unconvinced.

"You seem out of it." She was sure he just wanted to leave. "We won't have to stay much longer."

"Haylee. For one, of course, we will be one of the last ones to leave. It's your best friend's wedding after all. And two, I'm fine with that. I'm having a good time, so stop worrying."

Yielding, she vowed to drop it. After a moment's silence, Pete told her, "I love you."

It wasn't the first time he had said it, but hearing those words from him still cinched her heart every time. For reasons she couldn't fully explain to him, she hadn't been able to say it back as yet. A part of her had rebuilt the wall that had been erected prior to Scott, and she feared simply being open to love again would cause history to repeat itself. She was trying so hard to be cautious, to be sensible about a relationship with him, but her heart was letting her fail at those things. Perhaps it was because deep down, she knew this time would be different.

With the romance and promises of commitment in the air all around her, her guard was down enough to let her speak freely.

"I love you too." She leaned in to kiss him lightly,

swallowing the ball of nerves in her throat beforehand. With that, she was delighted to feel her initial fear subside, being replaced with a calm certainty that what she said and felt was *right*.

Some of Pete's tension eased, but he wanted to probe further. "You know I care about you deeply, don't you?"

"Yes. Yes, I do."

He nodded. "And you know that I'd never hurt you? I'd always treat you right."

Haylee tipped her head back up from his shoulder to look him square on. "Somehow, I know this to be true." She was tempted to ask why he was saying all this, but she didn't want to spoil the moment. When you got a man to open his heart to you, she thought it might be best to not do anything that would make him hold back the next time.

"Good. I'm glad you do."

They finished their dance pulled in tight to one another, but their moment together was short-lived. Haylee was pulled away with the other bridesmaids to dance after the music once again picked up the pace. Pete watched as she spun around the dance floor with the other women, and then as she spoke with numerous members of Kathy's family. He kept his promise by patiently waiting for her as one by one people trickled out the door to leave.

The room was still half full as Haylee stood next to Kathy.

"My mom just told me our limo is waiting outside. The DJ said he would announce our departure so I wouldn't have to try to say good-bye to everyone one by one. But I'm glad I have a minute to say good-bye to you. Thanks again for everything."

Kathy gave her hug.

"Congratulations. Even though I know I've said it a couple times already."

196

Kathy gave her a wide grin. "Thanks."

"Should I stay to help with anything? Do you need me to remove the centerpieces or your gifts there in the corner?"

"No, my parents said they will stay until all the guests have left and will take everything that needs to go." She looked at one of the floral centerpieces, a mix of the red roses that were in her bouquet, along with burnt orange calla lilies and white hydrangeas. Most of them had been taken by guests as requested by the bride. "Make sure you grab one of the remaining centerpieces. They should last for at least another week or so."

"I will. They will look great on my dining room table, as they did here." She paused. "Have fun on the honeymoon. I hear it's the best part."

Kathy closed her eyes as she imagined the pictures of St. Lucia and the waves of the ocean lapping up on the shore in front of their hotel. "I can't wait to sit on my butt and relax after this wedding whirlwind." She looked at Haylee again. "Now go get Pete and get out of here. The night is still young."

She was trying to be subtle because she didn't want to give anything away, but it was hard to hide her excitement for her friend. Pete had sought out Kathy's advice, so she knew what the rest of the evening held for Haylee.

Haylee glanced over to see Pete's nose buried in a glass of what looked to be scotch or whiskey, turned herself in that direction. "Call me when you get back," she said before she left.

Haylee made her way first toward Pete, motioning for him to follow her, then toward the elevators so the two of them could go up to the room they had for the night. Several rooms had been reserved for guests of the wedding at a discounted rate, and since both of their homes were a decent drive away, they opted to take advantage of the deal. This way they didn't have to worry about being too tired to drive.

Pete caught up with her after retrieving the coat he had almost forgotten he had walked in with. He felt scatterbrained, and it would have been quite the tragedy to have left that coat behind. Haylee had already summoned the elevator down, but Pete insisted they go for a walk together first.

"Alright, but let me go change first. It has to be pretty chilly out there by now, and I am very ready to get out of this dress."

Pete pulled her back as the elevator doors chimed open. He hadn't considered that she would want to change, and it wasn't part of the plans he had made. He didn't want her to see the rose petals he had scattered in the room before dinner had started, while the wedding party had been busy taking pictures, or the champagne he had on ice for what he hoped would be a celebration. No, that was to be discovered later.

"How about you slip on my coat? We won't be long." Anticipating her next question, he said, "I'll be fine, I was outside not too long ago and it isn't too bad out."

Resigned, she took his coat and followed him out the door. He had been right. It was an unseasonably warm evening, with the smell of fallen leaves in the air. The hour was early enough that the streets were still littered with people going about their business. The moon shone bright in the sky without a cloud in sight, accompanied by brilliant stars. Haylee clasped Pete's hand as they walked, glad he had suggested they go out for some air before going to bed.

She was touched when they reached their destination. She sat beside him on the bench next to the river, admiring the light from building windows reflecting off of the water.

"You first said you loved me here."

He took a seat beside her. "Glad you remembered."

"A lady doesn't forget." They had gone to dinner at a restaurant about a block away, then had stopped in this spot on the way back to the car. The night had been clear and serene, like this one was, and it warmed her heart to remember the sincerity with which he had told her how he felt about her.

They sat for a moment in silence, taking in the scenery.

Pete worked up his courage and told her, "I brought you here for a reason."

Haylee lifted her head off his shoulder. "Oh?"

"I wanted to talk about our future."

Butterflies of nerves fluttered about in her stomach. This wasn't sounding good. She knew something had been wrong with him all day. "Our future?" She had already started to brace herself for something along the lines of 'I love you, but I don't see this working out in the long run' or similar words.

Instead, he bent down in front of her traditionally, on one knee. He began, "Attending weddings can usually have you thinking one of two things. They either have you questioning if the person you are with could really be the one you could marry, or they strengthen your conviction that you will be next to walk down the aisle. As I watched you all day, it became even more clear that we should always be together, even more so than when I bought you this."

He pulled the small black box out of the inside pocket of the coat Haylee wore, and opened it. She couldn't even tell it was there.

The ring sparkled as radiantly as the stars above. The

emerald-cut center diamond was flanked by baguettes of the same shape, and the stones were crystal clear.

"I was nervous and hesitant because I wasn't positive on how you felt. But when we were dancing, you eased my tension. I want you to be my wife Haylee. Will you marry me?"

Mouth still agape, words of response were frozen in her throat. Of all things, this question was the last she had expected. She forced herself to snap out of it, to lift her gaze from the box to his face.

The joy that was bursting inside her slowly spread to reveal itself as an expression on her face. Her hands came up to cover her mouth in shock then reached out to touch Pete's cheeks.

"Yes. Yes, I will. Of course."

Relief coursed through his system as he let out the breath he had been holding while waiting for her to respond. He met her lips, pressed them hard against hers, then embraced her with all the force the kiss had had.

When they finally peeled away from each other, he took the ring from its velvet perch, slipped it on her finger. It glided down smoothly with little resistance and proved itself to be a perfect fit.

Haylee admired the symbol of promise and then her new fiancée. And knew without doubt that the two of them would be a perfect fit as well.